W9-DFV-965

THE MISSING

THE MISSING

MELANIE FLORENCE

JAMES LORIMER & COMPANY LTD., PUBLISHERS
TORONTO

Canadian edition published in 2016.
United States edition published in 2017.

All blackbird chapter titles are quotes from songs, poems and nursery rhymes including Lynyrd Skynyrd, Peggy Lee, The Beatles, Alfred Tennyson, Wallace Stevens, and "Sing a Song of Sixpence."

James Lorimer & Company Ltd., Publishers acknowledges the support of the Ontario Arts Council. We acknowledge the support of the Canada Council for the Arts which last year invested $24.3 million in writing and publishing throughout Canada. We acknowledge the Government of Ontario through the Ontario Media Development Corporation's Ontario Book Initiative.

Canada

Cover design: Tyler Cleroux
Cover image: Shutterstock, iStock

Library and Archives Canada Cataloguing in Publication

Florence, Melanie, author
The missing / Melanie Florence.

Issued in print and electronic formats.
ISBN 978-1-4594-1088-6 (bound).--ISBN 978-1-4594-1085-5 (pbk).--
ISBN 978-1-4594-1086-2 (epub)

I. Title.

PS8611.L668M569 2016 jC813'.6 C2015-907196-8
C2015-907197-6

James Lorimer &
Company Ltd., Publishers
117 Peter St., Suite 304
Toronto, ON, Canada
M5V 2G9
www.lorimer.ca

Canadian edition
(978-1-4594-1085-5)
distributed by:
Formac Lorimer Books
5502 Atlantic Street
Halifax, NS, Canada
B3H 1G4

American edition
(978-1-4594-1088-6)
distributed by:
Lerner Publishing Group
1251 Washington Ave N
Minneapolis, MN, USA
55401

Printed and bound in Canada.
Manufactured by Friesens Corporation in Altona, Manitoba, Canada in May 2016.
Job # 222750

For my family — Chris, Josh and Taylor

PROLOGUE
WHERE SOMEBODY WAITS . . .

He was always surprised at how quiet it got by the water at night. Further down, junkies were getting high on whatever they could find to get them through another night on the streets. Beyond them, prostitutes looked for one more date. But in his little spot on the riverbank, he couldn't hear the street noises or the other people escaping their lives for the night. The shadows hid him. Lost in the darkness. Waiting.

He stood close enough to her to smell her perfume. To hear her breathe. Cloaked in shadow, he could observe her without her noticing.

He watched as she checked her phone. She tossed it into her bag when she didn't find what she was hoping for. She sighed, picking her phone up again and typing out a message before putting it back. She closed her eyes and leaned against the cold concrete wall.

Despite the chill in the air and the dampness that seeped into his own bones, he saw her starting to doze off, her long, jet-black hair falling forward and hiding her face. Silly little blackbird, he thought. This is no place to sleep.

He shifted his weight and then took a step towards her. Somewhere in the depths of her exhaustion, she registered the sound of footsteps, dully echoing off the concrete. He cleared his throat and watched her eyes open wide. She pressed her back against the wall, slid down and pulled her knees up against her chest, wrapping her thin arms tightly around them. The street lights didn't even begin to pierce the shadows down here. He stopped just outside of her line of vision and watched as she held her breath, trying not to make a sound. Trying not to move. He could almost hear her heart beating furiously in her chest like a bird's wings.

He flipped open his lighter and lit his cigarette, smiling as she jumped at the sudden burst of light. She tried to shrink further away from him and search for a weapon of some kind. She wouldn't find one. He had already checked. He drew on the cigarette, the end flaring bright orange and illuminating his face for a moment. She breathed a sigh of relief as she recognized him.

He stepped towards her, smiling. "I was hoping I might find you here."

CHAPTER 1
GIRL GONE

I heard the buzz of excited chatter following me up the hallway before I was even halfway to my locker. Kids were standing in groups, their heads together over their phones, basically climbing over each other to see what was probably some lame recap of a WB show. Not surprising — it was high school after all. But there was something different about the buzz this time. There was a desperate excitement to it. I was half-listening and half-wishing I had stopped for a mochaccino on my way to school, so I managed to catch only bits and pieces of conversation through my usual Monday morning haze.

"Did you hear?"

"Oh my God! Yes!"

"Do you know her?"

"Yes she's in my gym class . . ."

"We were really good friends in grade seven . . ."

"What do you think happened to her?"

I made my way to my locker, dropped my backpack on the floor and reached for my lock. I swung the locker door open just as Mia strode up and leaned heavily onto the locker beside me.

"Did you hear?" she asked, picking up the backpack.

I took it from her and started unpacking my books. "Hear what?"

Mia stared at me, her mouth hanging open. "You can't be serious? Everyone's talking about it!"

"About what?" I was searching my locker for my English book and only half-listening.

Mia grabbed the books out of my hand. "Feather! Get your head out of your ass!"

I shuddered. "I hate that saying, Mia!"

"Oh my God." Mia shook her head. "Would you listen? Carli's missing."

I looked up sharply. "What? What do you mean by missing? Is that what everyone's talking about?"

"Yeah. She was supposed to meet Ben on Saturday. They were going to a movie and she didn't show up. Turns out Ben was the last one who talked to her the night before. He tried to reach her all weekend but she didn't answer." She paused and took a breath, then plunged on. "So Ben goes over to Carli's place and her foster mom said she was with a friend . . . who doesn't exist!"

"What do you mean, doesn't exist?" I asked.

"Ben has no clue who she could have been with. He thought she was at the rec centre. No one has heard from her since."

I stopped and stared at her, dumbstruck. Carli and I had grown up together. We weren't as close as we used to be; she hadn't spent a Saturday night at my house in awhile, but I still considered her a friend.

"So no one has heard from her?" I asked. Mia shook her head.

"Not since Friday night. And the police aren't doing anything."

I was outraged — and terrified for Carli. But given the history of the police with the Aboriginal community, I wasn't that surprised. Carli was a foster kid. We all knew to the police that equalled a high-risk, unwanted kid who got what she deserved. It made me sick. I watched the news. Aboriginal women were going missing or being killed across the country and the police just ignored it and turned a blind eye.

A group of girls passed us in the hallway, talking loudly.

"I heard she was giving blow jobs for twenty bucks down by the riverbank," one girl said, smirking.

"Well, I heard she went down to that rec centre to score drugs. Probably got a bad batch of meth or something," a tall blonde with a pixie cut cackled to her friends. "Aren't all those Indians on drugs?" My face coloured and I grabbed Mia's arm as she lunged towards them.

"We're not all on drugs, bitch. But we do all know how to hunt. Remember that," Mia yelled at the retreating group.

"I don't know how to hunt," I commented dryly.

Mia grunted at me, pushing the hair out of her face and glaring down the hallway at the girls.

"Do you know how to hunt?" I asked Mia, trying to distract her.

Mia glanced back at me and smirked. "Oh shut up. Of course not. I was born in St. Boniface and grew up in Osborne Village. I don't get back to the rez too often."

I closed my locker and nudged my friend as the bell rang.

"Come on, Mia. We're going to be late for English."

"Oh shit." Mia looked at me sideways as she linked her arm through mine. "So what's this book about? Just a quick summary. We've got three minutes."

I managed to give Mia enough info on the reading

assignment to fake her way through class and even answer a question fairly intelligently. But watching Mia bullshit her way through English wasn't enough to distract me from Carli's disappearance. I found myself watching the clock, counting the minutes until class ended and I could meet up with Jake.

The lunch bell rang shrilly, followed by the chaos of hundreds of students barrelling down the hall towards the cafeteria and the promise of greasy french fries and cheesy pizza. I had listened to my classmates speculate about Carli's disappearance all morning. Even kids who knew Carli, and should have known better, talked about her as if she was some drug-addled, alcohol-fuelled hooker who got what she deserved. Even worse were the whispers about Carli's boyfriend, Ben. People said Ben was responsible for her disappearance. Or murder, depending who you talked to.

Skipping the crowded lunch line, I wove through the tables to where Jake was sitting, completely immersed in a book. I leaned over and kissed his cheek.

"What are you reading?" I asked, smiling at the familiar frown my boyfriend always wore when he was reading. He glanced up with a smile.

"*Silence of the Lambs.* I can't believe I never got around to reading this before." He studied me as I sat down. "So you heard about Carli?" he asked gently, pushing his blond hair out of his eyes. He always seemed to need a haircut, I thought fondly.

"Yeah. I don't know what's true, though," I admitted, sighing deeply. "Everyone has a different story. She's missing. She's dead. Ben had something to do with it. What actually happened?"

A flash of anger passed over my boyfriend's handsome

face. "I've known Ben since kindergarten. He loves Carli. He'd never do anything to hurt her. He cried when we had to dissect frogs in grade seven!" I smiled at that. "I called him earlier. He said she's definitely missing but that's all he knows. I guess she was down by the Riverwalk again."

I nodded. It was a well-known fact that Carli liked to escape down to the river when it got too loud at her foster home. She had a spot in Bonnycastle Park where she liked to sit and read. Or she'd hang out with other kids by the Midtown Bridge; some of them homeless, some just taking a break like her. Then she'd usually get a hot meal and a bed at the rec centre at night.

"Did the cops say anything to Ben about what they think happened?" I asked.

Jake shook his head. "They're not being very helpful. They said she's a habitual runaway even though everyone told them that she's never run away before. She just goes down to the rec centre for a break. She always comes back. And the longest she's ever been gone is two days." He brushed his hair back again. "This is the third day she's been gone. She's not answering her phone, and Ben says even when she's down by the river, she always answers her phone. He doesn't know what happened to her but he's freaking out."

"Yeah, I bet," I replied, rubbing Jake's arm.

"She's my lab partner this year, you know," Jake told me absently, his face pale.

"I didn't know that. I'm sure she's fine, Jake." I laced my fingers through his on top of the table.

He looked at me, his face serious. "Are you? Because Carli isn't the first girl in this city to go missing, you know."

I did know.

"The first Aboriginal girl, you mean?" I asked pointedly.

Jake nodded. "Yeah. She's not the first Aboriginal girl to go missing." He sighed. "She's been in how many foster homes? You'd think she'd have gained some street smarts."

"What do you mean?" I asked, bristling.

"Nothing," he responded. "Except, what exactly was she doing on the Riverwalk at night?"

"What are you getting at?"

"Nothing," he repeated. "It's just . . . usually it's a certain kind of person who hangs out down there at night."

I gaped at him. "What? Are you saying you think she was asking for something to happen to her?"

"No, of course not."

"Then don't say things like that!" I was furious. He held his hands up.

"I'm sorry. It's just that I've been down there at night and it's not safe."

"I know," I said. "But still." Jake enveloped me in a hug.

"Sorry, Feather. I am. I like Carli. I hope she's okay."

"Yeah," I told him, taking a fry off his plate. "Me too." I paused for a second. "Wait, what were you doing on the Riverwalk at night?" I asked.

"Nothing," Jake said. He didn't meet my eyes as he opened his book again.

I thought the conversation was over when he looked up at me. "Just promise me you'll be careful, Feather," he begged. "Promise you won't go anywhere alone. At least until they catch whoever took Carli."

CHAPTER 2
MYSTERIOUS

I couldn't take it all in. First, I find out a girl I know is missing. Then my boyfriend tells me he thinks someone took her.

"How do you know someone took her?" I asked. "The cops haven't said anything, have they? Maybe she just took off for a while."

"She wouldn't, Feather. Not without telling Ben."

Mia appeared and threw herself down into the seat beside Jake, swiping a few fries from his plate.

"Not without telling Ben what?" she asked, shoving Jake's fries into her mouth. Jake pushed his tray over to her.

"Help yourself," he said. "Carli wouldn't take off without telling Ben where she was going and when she'd be back."

Mia nodded. "He's right, Feather. I know Carli. Something happened to her or she would have called Ben."

"So what do you think happened to her? Where is she? Why haven't the police found her?" I asked.

"I don't know, obviously," Mia answered. "But I'm sure she'll show up. Carli's tough."

"Yeah, she is." Jake smiled. The bell rang harshly and I jumped, knocking my drink over. Jake grabbed it and threw a crumpled napkin over the spill. "I'll meet you at your locker after school, okay? Mia, do you need a lift home?"

She stuffed a few more fries in her mouth and shook her head. "Nah. I drove my mom's car today."

Jake nodded. "Okay. Just be careful. Both of you."

"Yes, Dad." Mia rolled her eyes. Jake tossed a ketchup packet at her and held out his hand to me.

"I'll walk you to class," he said. I stood up and took his hand.

"I'll come over after dinner," I told Mia, who saluted in return.

"And I'll try to stay out of trouble until then," she said.

× × ×

The rest of the day passed in a blur of classes and a constant stream of gossip and innuendo about Carli. I had heard it all by now. The hooker allegations. The rumours about Carli's rampant drug use. The theory that Ben killed Carli in a jealous or drunken rage and threw her in the river. The speculation that some crazy serial killer of First Nations women grabbed her and was holding her hostage as a sex slave until he got bored and hacked her to pieces. I just wanted to get my stuff from my locker and escape the chatter for a while.

Jake was waiting at my locker, deeply immersed in his novel.

"Did they solve the mystery?" I asked, walking up behind him. He turned slowly, smiling down at me, his finger marking his place in the book. I stood on my toes and kissed him, slowly and sweetly. Closing my eyes and breathing in the familiar scent of him. Cologne and books and cinnamon gum.

"Rough day, huh?" he asked, hugging me tightly against him. I nodded into his chest.

"Let's just get out of here, okay? Please?" I pleaded. He grabbed my bag and wrapped an arm around me.

"Yeah, let's go."

The walk to the car was quiet. Both of us were deep in thought. I was worried about Carli but also outraged about the horrible things everyone was saying about her. Carli kept to herself for the most part. It pissed me off that no one knew what they were talking about. And Jake was having trouble accepting that the funny, quiet girl who cracked little side jokes to him during Chemistry, who was one of the smartest girls he knew but who never spoke up in class, was missing. Maybe worse than missing.

I looked over at him as we reached his car. "You okay?" I asked, squeezing his hand. He looked down at me and I could tell by his face that he was imagining all of the horrible things that could take me away from him. He kissed the top of my head.

"Yeah, I'm fine." He opened the car door and closed it carefully behind me. The drive home was as quiet as the walk to the car had been. I cleared my throat.

"So, do you have a lot of homework?" I asked. Seriously? I thought to myself. That's the best you can come up with? I sighed as he smiled at me and reached for my hand.

"It's okay, Feather," he said, kissing my knuckles and giving me goosebumps. "We don't have to talk." I smiled gratefully at him and looked out the window for the rest of the ride.

As the car pulled onto my street, I saw a familiar white Sunfire sitting in my driveway. I sat up straight.

"Hey!" I exclaimed. "Kiowa's home!" My older brother

was away at school, and although the University of Winnipeg was a stone's throw from our place, he hadn't been home very often. He preferred to stay in his dorm or hang out at the library, reading some dusty, old book about chemistry or anatomy. He said it gave him the "real college experience." I always suspected it was just an excuse to get away from a house full of sometimes moody women. I turned to Jake.

"Are you coming in?"

He shook his head.

"I can't. I have to pick my mom up. But I'll call you later, okay? We can do math homework together on the phone. It'll be fun." I leaned over and kissed him. He sighed and touched my face softly.

"I worry about your idea of fun sometimes, Jake." I smiled and jumped out the door, blowing a kiss over my shoulder, eager to get inside and see my brother.

I threw the door open and dropped my backpack on the floor, looking into the living room. Kiowa wasn't there. I headed into the kitchen. Nothing. I heard his voice coming from the back deck and headed towards it. He was slouching in a lounge chair, a glass of iced tea beside him and a huge smile on his face as he spoke into his cell phone. I stopped suddenly, not wanting to interrupt when I heard him talking in a sweet voice that was unlike my brother's usually serious tone.

"I know. I missed you too. I can't get away until late. Maybe ten?"

I frowned. Last I heard, Kiowa had broken up with his horrible Barbie doll girlfriend, Mindi. Yes, her name was actually Mindi. With an "i" that she dotted with little hearts. Mindi was a giggly, annoying girl who wore shirts that were too tight and skirts that were too short. I had literally danced around the room when I heard that I wouldn't be subjected to Mindi's vapid company anymore. But he was obviously talking to a girl. I opened the patio door and stepped out. Kiowa glanced up at me. He looked like a deer caught in the headlights for a second, but he quickly recovered and smiled brightly.

"Hey, sis. My sister's here. I've gotta run. Yeah. See you later." He hung up his phone and stood up, opening his arms wide. "Get over here, kid." I stepped in for a hug.

"So who was that? And please don't tell me it was Mindi." I shuddered dramatically. Kiowa laughed.

"No, it most definitely was not Mindi. Just a buddy from school."

"But . . ." My curiosity was getting the better of me. It didn't sound like he was talking to a buddy to me, but Kiowa cut me off quickly.

"So how was school? Anything new and exciting happening in suburbia?" he asked.

"Well, a girl in my grade went missing over the weekend," I told him, sitting down in one of the deck chairs and sliding my shoes off so I could tuck my feet underneath me.

Kiowa frowned. "I'm sorry, Feather. I heard about that. It was Carli, right?"

"Yeah. I still can't believe she's missing. She's Jake's lab partner this year so he's shook up too. We know her boyfriend, Ben, pretty well. How did you hear about it?"

He shrugged and looked away. "When I was out earlier, I overheard some people talking about it. So do they have any idea what happened to her?"

I shrugged. "From what Jake heard, the cops aren't too interested in a missing Indian girl. She sometimes takes a few days away from her foster home when it gets to be too loud or too much. They don't believe she's really missing and won't take it seriously. I don't know." I shook my head. "It's infuriating."

Kiowa nodded. "Yeah. I was just telling . . . Mom . . . that she should be careful. Especially down by the Red. It's gotten kind of sketchy down there lately. You need to be careful too, Feather. Don't go down there alone, okay?"

"I don't hang out down there, Kiowa. But I'll be careful." I settled back onto my chair and reached for his iced tea. I took a long gulp. "So how's school?"

CHAPTER 3
HOME

Kiowa leaned back in his chair, putting his feet up on the table beside me. I shoved them off immediately.

"Hey!" he laughed. "School's fine. We've been talking about the Body Farm in pathology class."

"The what?" I asked.

"It's a research facility in Knoxville where they study the process of decomposition on the human body under different conditions."

"What! Why? That's disgusting!" I shuddered.

"To help solve murders. It's fascinating."

"It's repulsive," I told him.

"But it's . . ."

"Nope!" I interrupted. "Not interested. Come on." I smacked him on the leg. "Come help me with dinner."

I didn't get how my brilliant brother could be so fascinated by the thought of studying rotting corpses. It was bad enough listening to him go on and on about whatever dead thing they happened to be dissecting in class, which he took pictures of in far too much detail. It was disturbing. I smacked him again.

Kiowa hauled himself up and followed me into the kitchen where he started to bang pots and pans together while doing absolutely nothing to help. At least he distracted me from Carli's disappearance with his non-stop monologue about what he was dissecting in anatomy. I threw the corn in the boiling water while he rambled on about holding a heart.

In typical "mom" fashion, mine blew in the door at exactly 5:30, calling my name before she was even inside. She threw her purse, missing the table entirely.

"Feather!" she shriek-yelled at me.

"In here," I called back from the kitchen where Kiowa and I were getting dinner ready.

My mother, all five feet and two inches of her, nearly sent me to the floor with a hug that felt like a linebacker had hit me in the solar plexus.

"Hi, Mom," I patted her on the back. "Ki's home." I raised my eyebrows at him over my mom's head.

"Are you okay, honey?" my mom asked. "I heard about Carli. God, I can't believe this is happening. That poor girl." She looked over my shoulder. "Hi, Kiowa."

"Hi, Mom." He waved at her as she clung to me.

"Listen, Feather," she said as she held me at arm's length, studying my face. "Aboriginal women are four times more likely to be murdered than non-Aboriginal women."

My mom was the head of marketing for a major hotel chain. She was big on throwing numbers at me but this one freaked me out.

"Are you serious?" I asked her.

"That can't be right, Mom," Kiowa called out, carrying a platter of chicken into the dining room.

"It is right. And you really need to be careful, Feather," she said.

"I'm always careful, Mom."

"You should be careful too, you know, Mom," Kiowa interjected. I looked over at him, then at my mother.

Small as she was, it had never occurred to me that she might be in any danger. My father left us before I was born, so all I had ever known was that my mom could handle anything. She had worked hard to give us a good home while putting herself through school, and then she worked her way up through the hotel ranks. My mom was the strongest woman I knew. She always worried about me but rarely worried about herself. I hadn't considered the danger she might be in.

"Is that really true?" I asked, my heart suddenly beating faster as I thought about the nights she worked late and walked to her car in a dark parking lot by herself. "Four times more likely?"

She picked up the bowl of potatoes while I grabbed the corn and followed Kiowa to the table. She pulled out her chair and settled into it with a sigh.

"Yes. Sadly, it is." She helped herself to a chicken breast. "You really do need to be careful, okay?"

I nodded and she smiled at Kiowa.

"You should have told me you were coming home, Ki! How long are you staying?" she asked. "I've got a break before the next term starts," he told her. "I put it on the calendar for you." He gestured towards the kitchen.

"Right. I forgot. " she told him.

"Which is why you have the calendar, Mom." He smiled at her and she instantly smiled back. She never could resist her little boy.

"Okay, okay. More time for you to spend with your old mom," she said.

"As long as my mom is careful out there too," he told her,

pointedly. “And you’re not old.” I nodded in agreement, my mouth full of potatoes and corn.

“Always,” she replied, smiling. She glanced over at me. “I’m sure they’ll find Carli, sweetie.”

“I hope so,” I said, helping myself to another piece of chicken.

She smiled softly, then turned to my brother again.

“So tell me about your classes, Kiowa.”

× × ×

Normally I love driving. Kiowa left me his old car when he started university, and he tricked it out with an awesome sound system for my birthday. Sometimes I just cruised around and listened to music. Usually it relaxed me but I was edgy tonight. Warnings from your boyfriend, brother and mom will do that to you.

The light turned red and I pulled to a stop, tapping my fingers on the dashboard to the music while I waited. Mia’s house was about five minutes away, but as the light turned green, I somehow found myself turning towards the riverfront. It wasn’t a place where I hung out very often but I had taken Mia some clothes down there once when she was avoiding going home for a day or two. I went to the rec centre with her to keep her company once or twice. But that was pretty much the extent of my experience at the river at night.

During the day, the Riverwalk was full of tourists and people visiting The Forks. It was a vastly different world at night. Just steps from The Forks was an area you didn’t want to find yourself in at night. But some girls, like Mia and Carli, hung out there with absolutely no fear. It was a local hangout for kids who couldn't get a bed at the rec centre for the night or who just wanted to hang out and escape their lives for a little while. I never got the appeal. Then again, I was lucky. Sure, a single mother had raised me, but she loved us more than life itself. As uncool as it may sound, I had always hoped to be just like her when I grew up. She was strong, confident and perfectly happy with herself. She didn't need a man to fill some void in her life like Mia's mom. My mom, brother and I were always close. We were an anomaly. Especially in our neighbourhood where alcoholism and domestic violence were much more common than a happy, stable family.

Carli hadn't seen either of her parents for years. She had been shuttled from one foster home to the next for the past ten years, while her mother did time for peddling meth. Not one was a real home, but at least her current foster mom was cool and seemed to actually care. She used to tell me stories of the people who were supposed to take care of her. She was kicked out of her last foster home when the man of the house tried to get into her bed in the middle of the night. Carli had pulled a knife on him.

Mia's family wasn't much better. Her dad died of a drug overdose years ago. Mia was the one who had found him. Her mother mostly ignored her and paraded man after useless man through their lives until she settled for Leonard. Let's just say Leonard wasn't really father material.

The closer I got to the river, the sketchier it looked. Women wore little more than the makeup on their faces, which did nothing to disguise how strung out they were. They stood around and called out to one another, leaning against anything they could find to hold themselves up. An angry-looking man who had to be at least six foot seven walked across the street in front of me and flipped me off. I slammed on the brakes to keep from hitting him, sure he'd leave a dent in my hood and then walk away unscathed. I watched him reach the opposite sidewalk, his steroid-enhanced muscles straining against his black T-shirt.

Shaking my head, I stepped on the gas as the hookers cackled on their corner. I cruised closer to the rec centre. I found myself glancing at the group of kids huddled outside, smoking and yelling obscenities at one another. At least three-quarters of them were Indigenous. Not surprising in this neighbourhood.

My heart raced as I caught a glimpse of a girl dressed all in black, her long hair braided down her back. Carli. I hit the brakes, and as the car behind me honked wildly, the kids turned around to stare. Then I saw the girl who was definitely not Carli. She laughed as the person behind me honked again.

What was I doing down here? I had hoped against hope that Carli was out here somewhere, waiting for someone to find her. Maybe someone had jacked her phone or something so she couldn't call Ben and no one could reach her? My cell dinged with a text and I jumped. That was kind of creepy. I glanced down at my phone, sitting on the passenger seat. Mia. I was supposed to meet her fifteen minutes ago. I looked over at the kids once more. They dressed mostly in black, just like Carli and Mia usually dressed. Then I turned the steering wheel and headed away from the waterfront.

CHAPTER 4
FOUR AND TWENTY BLACKBIRDS

They were all the same. A tribe of discontented youth milling around in their black clothes like a shambling group of the undead. Or a flock of crows. Or the unlucky blackbirds from that old song his mother used to sing to him.

Are you so unhappy with your sad little lives that you're willing to risk losing them, little blackbirds?

Life is short, he ruminated. His gaze rested on one girl in particular. She was different from the rest of them.

Some lives are shorter than others are, he thought.

CHAPTER 5
DADDY ISSUES

"I am so sorry!" I called out as soon as Mia answered her door. She rolled her eyes at me and stood aside to let me in.

"Where the hell were you?" she asked, shoving me casually with her shoulder as I walked past her.

"I went for a drive."

Mia looked at me quizzically. There's a reason we've been best friends for years. We balance each other and we can pretty much read each other's minds. She always knows when not to push and this was obviously one of those times. I didn't mind telling her about my jaunt down to the river but not while standing just inside her front door where anyone could hear us. She nodded but didn't say another word about it as I walked into the kitchen.

"So, Leonard's home," she whispered, rolling her eyes again. "He's snoring on the couch, so hopefully we can get into my room without waking him up." Leonard was a nasty drunk who, instead of getting angry when he drank, got friendly. Too friendly. Inappropriately friendly. Especially when Mia's mom was at work. Her mom worked two jobs to support Mia and Leonard: one cleaning rooms at a motel and one slinging drinks at a dive bar. She was rarely home. When she was, she didn't take much notice of her daughter.

I tiptoed over to the fridge and grabbed a couple of Diet Cokes while Mia plucked a bag of barbeque chips out of the cupboard.

"Come on," I stage-whispered to her, heading towards the kitchen door on my toes, humming the "Pink Panther" theme song. Mia frowned.

"I think we have M&M's somewhere. Hang on." She opened a cupboard and rustled around inside.

"Shhh!" I cautioned, glancing towards the living room.

"Can you check that one?" She gestured towards another cupboard, her hands still deep in her own. "Where are they?"

I was gazing into a cupboard full of tea, coffee and, inexplicably, a bag of fist-sized marshmallows.

"What would you even use these for?" I asked Mia, holding them up. She stifled a giggle.

"I thought they'd make kick-ass s'mores."

"But where would you make s'mores?" I asked her. She was giggling louder now and it was contagious.

"I don't know! I just figured they'd be good to have. Just in case," she snorted.

"In case we ever went camping?" I asked, doubling over with laughter. "Hey, I know! Maybe we can put our hunting skills to use on that camping trip!"

Mia stood on her toes, trying to see the top shelf. We were still laughing and didn't hear her creepy stepdad ooze his way into the kitchen.

"Hey, ladies," he slurred. Mia turned quickly, her eyes wary. He was unsteady but it looked to me as if he was playing it up. Sure enough, he took a step towards Mia and then clumsily fake-tripped into her, his hand brushing against her breast. Mia pulled away and I felt my face burning.

"Hey, Leonard!" I called out, waving my hand in the air like an idiot, trying to distract him from Mia. "How's the job hunt going?" He looked away from Mia's chest and focused on me.

"I'm holding out for a management position." I started to laugh but then realized he was being serious. Wow. I'm sure his resumé consisted entirely of fry cook positions and gas station attendant jobs. He burped loudly and leaned in towards Mia. "At least I get to hang out with my girl." He leered, looking down into Mia's cleavage. She crossed her arms and stepped away from him.

"We're going to go study. Dinner is in the crockpot." She stepped around him and reached for my arm. We were close to a getaway when he reached out and cupped her ass. Mia jumped and I yelled before I could stop myself.

"Hey!" I shouted, stepping towards him and pushing Mia behind me. "Don't do that!"

This time he did laugh. "Oh, she doesn't mind, do you, Mia?" he asked, reaching around me and slapping her butt hard.

"Of course she does!"

Mia grabbed my arm and pulled me past Leonard. I glared at his smug face and considered smacking the smirk off it. Mia got me out of the kitchen and dragged me into her bedroom, closing the door behind us and locking it with a snap.

"That's new," I nodded towards the lock.

"Yeah, well . . . peace of mind. You know?" I did.

I cleared my throat. "So, umm, Leonard? He's getting pretty, ummm . . . ?" Mia was like a sister to me but there's no easy way to bring up what a perv your best friend's stepdad is.

"Friendly?" she asked, one eyebrow raised. "Handsy? How

about disgustingly effing gropey?"

"About that . . ." I smiled humourlessly at her. "He's getting a lot worse."

"Oh, you think?" she asked, a flash of anger crossing her face.

"You need to talk to your mom, Mia."

She sighed heavily and sat down on her bed. "I know, Feather. I've tried. But how do you tell your mom that her husband won't keep his hands off you? He never does it in front of her. He's a complete angel when she's around, which sadly, is almost never."

"She really has no idea?" I asked. How could she possibly miss the way he stared at Mia? It was disgusting. As if she was something the repulsive reptile wanted to devour. My skin was crawling at the thought. Poor Mia was stuck in the house with him. If her mother was the buffer between them, she was doing a horrible job.

"Nope. She thinks he's Mr. Wonderful. If Mr. Wonderful was unemployed and drank all her money away. It's fine, Feather. I can handle him."

"Mia! I just watched him grab your ass and brush against your chest like it was normal. What's he going to do next? Obviously you're worried if you put a lock on your door to keep him out." She wouldn't meet my eyes, so I knew I had hit the nail on the head. "He hasn't . . . done anything else, has he?" I blurted out.

"No! Of course not!" Her face was beet red.

"You have to tell your mom before he tries to, Mia. It'll be hard for her to hear, but you're her daughter. It's her job to protect you."

"Yeah." She didn't look convinced.

"Promise me you'll talk to her," I pleaded with her. I hated the idea that she had to stay in the same house with Leonard and his wandering hands.

"Okay, okay. I promise."

I leaned over to give her a hug.

"Good. I think it'll help, Mia. I really do."

"Yeah, maybe." Mia picked up her math textbook and flipped it open. "We should get this over with."

"Yeah. Okay. Listen, do you want to stay at my place for a day or two? Get away from the creeper out there?"

"No! I mean, no. If he keeps drinking, I'll just go to the rec centre or something." She smiled at me but it looked strained. She was acting so odd. Something was obviously up. Why was everyone acting so weird lately? It was like there was some big secret I wasn't in on.

I was confused, both by her quick refusal of my offer and by her willingness to put herself in danger. Did she feel so unsafe in her own home that she'd leave to go to the Riverwalk, which was even less safe? I glanced at the deadbolt on her bedroom door.

"You don't need to go to the rec centre, Mia. Come and stay with me. You need to be careful . . ." I trailed off. Because what can you possibly say that makes any sense of the fact that a seventeen-year-old girl — someone you know — has gone missing without a trace?

"I'm always careful, Feather."

"Yeah, well . . . so was Carli," I said pointedly.

"The rec centre is safe enough and I can always get a ride down there if I need to. My mom will be home tonight so I'll talk to her then. If there's a problem, I'll call you, okay?" She smiled at me and I nodded.

"Good. Okay. So bio, my least favourite of the homework genres," I opened my book with an exaggerated sigh, trying to lighten the mood while my mind raced, wondering who was driving her around. It wasn't me.

She threw a pillow at me and opened the bag of chips.

"And also my favourite. So what did you get for the first question?"

CHAPTER 6
THERE WAS A LITTLE BLACKBIRD

The first time he saw her, she was sitting on a bench outside the library. He watched her digging through her bag. It was a ridiculous, oversized thing that had to hurt when she slung it over her bird-like shoulder. She was delicate. He liked that. Like a little blackbird with her straight, glossy hair hanging down her back, soft as feathers. He'd love to brush it for her. To run his fingers through it and grab great handfuls . . . pulling her head back and exposing her neck to him.

She'd like that, he thought.

He hummed his mother's favourite song under his breath as he watched her pull a book out of her bag, opening it with slender fingers. She frowned when she read.

CHAPTER 7
GONE AND FORGOTTEN

"Is it just me, or is the schoolyard looking particularly empty today?" Mia asked. She wasn't wrong. The police had stopped hanging around and talking to people about Carli a week after she disappeared. The local reporters who had been lurking outside the school had found other stories to chase. Apparently, the retirement home's annual bingo festival made for more exciting news than a missing girl.

The halls were still ringing with gossip. But now it was about two senior boys, Matt and Dre, who had been caught making out in a car in the parking lot.

"I always knew he was gay!" I heard one girl tell her friends. "We dated for a week in junior high and he wouldn't kiss me. Totally called that one!"

People were unbelievable. Neither of the guys had shown up for school and I heard one was posting some suspiciously suicidal thoughts online. I knew both of them. Had always suspected they were gay. Never cared. They were nice guys and they didn't deserve the firestorm of attention they were getting just because the jackals at school needed to update their Instagram feeds with something new.

I swung into the guidance office on my way to my locker. Mr. Taylor was working on his book again, pecking away at his laptop with a look of deep concentration on his face.

"Hey, Mr. T."

He looked up and smiled. "What can I do for you, Feather?"

"So I know you heard about what happened in the parking lot, right?" I asked. He nodded. "Well, I heard Matt is putting some dark stuff online."

"Have you seen it yourself?" he asked me, concern written all over his face.

I shook my head. "No. But enough people are talking about it that I think it's probably true. My phone battery just died so I can't check but I thought maybe you could call his house? Maybe check on Dre too?"

"Can you show me?" he asked, turning his laptop towards me. I logged into my Instagram account and looked up Matt. I scanned his page quickly, and then wordlessly turned it back towards him.

"See? So can you call or something?" I asked. He read the page, his face serious.

He nodded. "Yeah, for sure. Thanks, Feather. I appreciate it."

I walked out of his office while he was dialing his phone and headed towards my locker, trying to tune out the gossip. Did people have nothing better to do than worry about everyone else's business? They were always looking for the next big thing to gossip about. I swerved left and went down the hall to the art room. I knew Mia would be there, working on some new crazy piece. I had tried unsuccessfully to find my inner artist alongside Mia, but I finally gave up this year after a kiln explosion that closed the art room for a week.

Sure enough, I found her standing in the art room with her back to the door. She was staring at a huge piece of paper taped to the wall, paintbrush in her mouth as she smeared a blotch of cobalt blue onto the surface with the side of her hand.

"Hey, Picasso," I called out from the doorway.

Mia took the brush out of her mouth and painted a bold stroke of deep purple in the middle. She answered without turning to look at me.

"What brings you to the art department? Bad morning?"

"Yeah." I picked up a lump of clay from one of the tables and mashed it between my fingers. "Everyone's talking about Dre and Matt. And no one's talking about Carli anymore. It bothers me that as soon as there's something else to gossip about, Carli is completely forgotten. But what about you? Did you talk to your mom yet?"

"Nope." She shook her head, a piece of hair coming out of the bun held in place with another paintbrush. "She didn't get home until after I fell asleep last night, and I left before she got up this morning." She saw the look on my face. "I'll talk to her tonight, Feather. I swear. She's not working tonight."

"Have you talked to Matt and Dre today?" I asked her, deftly changing the subject. Mia used to have a thing for Matt, and although they became really close friends, she never managed to turn it into anything more romantic. Given his love for Ryan Gosling movies and his ability to avoid sleeping with Mia despite everything she was doing to get him in her bed, I had suspected he was gay. Truthfully, though, he never tried very hard to hide his orientation. I'd be happy he was open about it now, except it was clearly destroying him.

"Yeah. I tried to call Matt but his phone was off. I've got a free period this morning. I've got my mom's car so I'm going to drive over," she said. "I heard what people are saying. His so-called friends are calling him a fag and saying he was giving Dre a blow job in his car."

"Seriously? What is this obsession? They were all saying Carli was giving blow jobs down at the riverfront too!" I replied. I was disgusted with the gossip and the innuendo by people who were supposed to be friends of Carli and now Matt and Dre.

"Well, she was, though." Mia looked up from her painting at me. I couldn't have been more shocked if Mia had told me she was stealing cars to finance her burgeoning art career.

"What are you talking about? Carli was nice! She wasn't some hooker, Mia!" I had known Carli all my life and I refused to believe it. She was so sweet and quiet.

"She did. Sometimes. It wasn't a regular thing for her or anything. But when she was desperate and needed a few bucks, she did what she had to do."

"Why didn't you ever tell me that?" I admit that I was shocked. I watched HBO as much as the next teenaged girl did. But this was someone I knew! She was someone the same age as me. I looked at Mia as something occurred to me. "Mia . . . you don't ever . . . when you stay down at the river, you haven't ever done . . . that . . . have you?"

"Feather, no! Of course not!" She shot me a look that told me what an idiot I was for even asking.

"Sorry. I'm sorry, Mia. I know you wouldn't. I just can't believe Carli would either."

Mia shrugged. "You don't get what it's like, Feather. You're lucky enough to have a stable home and a family who loves you. Not all of us are that lucky. Carli didn't have a home or a family. Sometimes you get desperate enough to do whatever it takes to survive. You know?"

The bell rang and Mia dropped her brushes into a tin can and pulled off her smock.

"I'm heading over to see Matt. I'll call you later, okay?" she said as she picked up her purse.

"Tell him to hang in there. He has people who care about him," I told her.

"Who cares about who?" Jake came up behind me and wrapped his arms around my waist, kissing my neck.

"Matt. Mia is heading over to see him now." I reached back and ran my fingers through his blond hair.

"Oh my God! Can you believe it? I've known Matt since we were kids and I had no idea." He paused for a second, thinking. "Wait, do you think he's been checking me out in the change room this whole time?"

I saw Mia's mouth drop open at the exact moment I pulled out of Jake's arms.

"What did you just say?" I asked.

"No offence or anything." He glanced between Mia and me. "But our showers don't have curtains. He probably watches me and the other guys all the time."

"Jake!" I was shocked. I had never seen this unattractive side of him before.

He put his hands up in front of him. "Look, I'm just saying what everyone else is thinking. I don't care who Matt wants to blow as long as he doesn't get all faggoty around me."

"I'm not standing here and listening to this. I need to see my friend." Mia threw her bag over her shoulder. "I'll call you later, Feather."

I stared hard at Jake. My perfect boyfriend. The other half of what my friends considered a perfect couple. I suspected I loved him, but how well did I actually know him?

CHAPTER 8
THROWAWAY LIVES

We didn't often get to have dinner together as a family anymore. My mom worked a lot of hours. With her usually working late and Kiowa away at school, I often spent dinners in front of the TV or reading in my room. Having all three of us home at once called for a big, home-cooked meal. We all pitched in. I chopped veggies for a salad while Kiowa barbecued steaks. My mom made dessert: homemade strawberry shortcake that looked delicious.

As we sat around the table and talked about Kiowa's classes, which neither my mother nor me actually understood, I couldn't help but think again about how different my home life was from Mia's. We both had single mothers but my mother had focused on raising my brother and me. She worked hard to provide for us, while Mia's mom paraded one useless boyfriend after another through Mia's life. Now she had to lock her bedroom door against her creepy molester stepfather. I knew if my mom ever brought home a guy who touched me like that, I could tell her and he'd be gone in a heartbeat. Probably with a black eye.

This led my thoughts back to Carli. She was shuttled from house to house and expected to fit in and not complain. I didn't know as much about what happened in her foster homes as I'm sure Ben did, but I knew she had been with a family who liked to hit their foster kids for any wrongdoing — real or imagined. I had seen her with black eyes and an arm in a cast. That wasn't even the worst situation she had been in. I couldn't imagine being Carli, moving from place to place and having to fly under the radar so you don't make waves. I couldn't conceive of a home where I didn't feel safe and secure with people looking out for me. What choice did she have but to find other kids like her and seek a refuge where they could all eat hot meals and not worry about being hurt or touched? It was starting to make sense. Not everyone had someone to talk to or count on. Not everyone had someone who worried about them.

"So the cops stopped coming around the school and no one is talking about Carli anymore," I blurted out, interrupting Kiowa's fascinating story about his latest physics lab. "Sorry," I said to him.

My mother sighed. "I assumed as much. There's an epidemic of missing and murdered women in Winnipeg — over a thousand murdered Indigenous women in this country and a hundred still missing — and a lot of people in power are ignoring it. They believe we're bringing it on ourselves. They think women in our community deserve to be victimized just because of the colour of our skin."

"How can they do that?" I asked, maybe naively. Not everyone lived as I did. But it seemed to me if a teenaged girl went missing, it was the duty of everyone to try to find her. "Why aren't they doing anything to find Carli . . . and all of those other women? Doesn't anybody care?" I was so worked up, so outraged that I was sweating. I wiped my forehead. "I just don't get it."

"Well, a lot of them are marginalized women. Prostitutes or homeless women. But I believe people are changing, especially in our community. After Winnipeg was named the most racist city in Canada, people started to address it. People are trying to do something about these women. Amnesty International, No More Stolen Sisters and the marches . . . it may not be what we'd like to see happen, but people are raising awareness." My mother looked at Kiowa and sighed. "There have been a lot of people passing the buck, refusing to take any responsibility or action. There have been calls for inquiries, but up to now, no one seemed to want to move forward with it. The government has left it to law enforcement to deal with. Women in our community are sexualized and seen as easy targets. Alcoholism has destroyed too many families and now women are often on their own. There's still a lot of racism directed towards us, both within and outside of law enforcement."

My brother applauded her speech and kissed her on the cheek. "Hear, hear! If Mom was in charge, we'd have a real roundtable organized in no time."

"I should be!" Mom was outraged.

"I think I know what you mean," I volunteered. "It's not just about Aboriginal girls after they go missing or are killed."

"Oh?" My mom looked over at me.

"Well, it happens a lot, doesn't it? Mia and I have men stopping their cars all the time and propositioning us when we're walking down the street and it's just as bad at the mall."

"What?" Kiowa looked furious suddenly. "When does this happen?"

"It happens all the time, Ki. They call us 'sexy little Indians' and they honk their horns. I guess I was offended but I didn't really think about it being racist. But they always seem to make some comment about us, like calling us 'squaws.'"

"That's awful, Feather." My mom reached over and took my hand.

"I've had it happen too," Kiowa admitted. "Not like that!" he interjected. "But when I was looking for a summer job, I had more than one person tell me they didn't feel they could trust me. I thought they meant because I was a kid. But one admitted it was because of my skin colour. It was humiliating."

I nodded. "I don't get why the local police aren't doing anything about Carli. She's still missing and they called off the search after a few days. There were plenty of people in the neighbourhood who would have kept looking but the police told them it wasn't necessary. They didn't find a thing. Not a clue. So why did they stop looking?"

"I don't know, Feather." My mother looked sad as she answered. "I really don't. I guess because Carli ran away before, they think she's run away again."

"But she wouldn't leave without telling Ben," I insisted.

My mom nodded. I knew she understood. I also knew she had to be worried about me. I worried about her too, since she was usually the last one to leave the office at night.

"You'll be careful, right, Mom?" I could tell she knew what I was thinking. She reached across the table and took my hands in hers.

"Of course. I usually walk out with Armando." Armando was one of the security guards at her office. "And you're being careful too, right?"

I nodded. "Definitely. I'm usually with Mia or Jake. Otherwise, I'm home." I looked over at Kiowa. "Hey, I'm sorry. I really brought this dinner down, didn't I? Why don't you tell us more about university? Maybe you can fill us in on the thrilling hours you spend in the lab? Are there any actual girls in that class?" I smirked at him, trying my best to lighten the mood. Kiowa and I had always been on the same wavelength. He smiled and started talking about . . . well, I think it was about physics but Kiowa is the only one in our family with a brain that processes numbers and theories easily. I inherited the more creative mentality of my mother. I played a couple of instruments and I loved to write. I'd swear Kiowa was adopted, except he looks just like the one picture of my dad that my mother left on the mantle.

"Fascinating as this is, I'm going to get the dessert. But keep talking, Ki. I'm sure I'll get the gist of it when I get back." I winked at him and stood up. The mood was lighter, Carli temporarily forgotten. Out of sight, out of mind, I found myself thinking. I immediately felt awful. I'd push the cops to keep looking the next time I saw them, I swore to myself. Maybe someone needed to remind them there were people who cared about our women. Even if she was just another Indian girl.

My phone dinged in the pocket of my hoodie. We had a strict "no phone" policy at the dinner table and my mother shot disapproving glances my way.

"I'm so sorry! I thought it was off," I swore.

"Turn it off now, please," my mom requested mildly, spooning more salad onto her plate. I nodded and reached for my phone. I glanced at the screen, purely by habit, and then stopped. I couldn't breathe. "Feather, what is it?"

I looked at my family, both of them staring at me with concern. I tried to take a breath and swallowed.

"It's from Jake. They found Carli. She's dead."

CHAPTER 9
THE REAL STORY

I didn't want to get up the next morning. I had barely slept. All I could think about was Carli — and how they had found her dead.

I *knew* her. I had heard her laugh and seen her kiss her boyfriend in the hallway. I had walked past her a million times. We sat together once in a while at lunch. I had invited her to my birthday parties when we were kids. Now I couldn't stop picturing her floating facedown in the river. Or beaten beyond recognition and lying somewhere on the Riverwalk. Or shot in the head and left to die in an alley. Suddenly every horror movie I had ever seen was running through my head. Then it struck me that I'd never again see her at school, holding hands with Ben. She was gone. Found in the river with her hair trailing behind her like underwater weeds.

I was jolted out of my thoughts when my mom knocked on the door.

"Feather?" she called.

"Yeah?" I answered.

She stuck her head in and gave me a concerned smile, dark circles like bruises under her eyes. "Just thought I'd see if you were up yet. Can I come in?" I nodded at her. She walked in and sat down heavily on the bed. She looked at me and brushed the hair off my face, tucking it behind my ear. "Did you get any sleep?" she asked.

I shook my head. "I couldn't stop picturing her in the river." My skin broke out in goosebumps thinking about it again.

"Yeah," she sighed, "me too. I still see her as that seven-year-old girl with her hair in braids who was afraid of balloons at your birthday party."

I smiled. "I forgot about that! She wouldn't play that game where you stood with a partner and squished the balloon between you to break it."

My mom laughed. "She spent the whole game upstairs in the kitchen with me."

"I know! Her partner was Melissa. She had to play by herself and was squishing her balloon against the wall!" It felt good to laugh for a minute but I immediately felt guilty for laughing when Carli would never laugh again. It must have been written all over me, because my mom took my face in her hands and smiled gently at me.

"It's okay to remember her, Feather. It's even okay to laugh and smile."

"Thanks, Mom." I hugged her. "I'll get ready."

"Is Jake picking you up?" Mom asked.

I paused, not meeting her eyes.

"I don't think so."

She touched my arm.

"Everything okay?"

"Yeah," I sighed. "He just said something that bothered me."

My mom laughed. "Oh, honey. Men tend to do that. You have to talk to him if he did something that bothered you. If you care about him, you have to communicate and work it out."

I nodded. "I'll try."

By the time I got into the shower and out the door, I felt a little better. I was still shook up about Carli, obviously, but at least I was slightly more awake. I hit the Tim Hortons drive-through for a large double double and a maple-dipped donut. My head hurt from crying. I needed the sugar and the caffeine badly if I was going to make it through what I already knew would be an awful day. I had no doubt that everyone had heard about Carli by now.

Sure enough, kids were huddled in groups from the parking lot to the front door. I parked my car and grabbed my bag out of the back seat, bracing myself for the onslaught of bullshit I knew was coming.

I was right. Teenagers live for gossip. What shocked me were the histrionics. I guess I shouldn't have been surprised. This school has more drama queens and phonies than the Kardashians.

I passed the most popular clique of girls on my way to the front entrance. Fiona, the red-haired leader, had collapsed against her friends, sobbing and crying the mascara off her face.

"What am I going to do without her?" she wailed as one of her friends patted her on the back. "She was my best friend!" She was crying so hard that I thought she might hyperventilate and pass out. I kind of hoped she would. Fiona hadn't said a word to Carli in two years, since Carli had kissed Fiona's boyfriend at a party. And they hadn't actually been close before that. But I was trying not to be cynical. Who knows? Maybe this was completely genuine.

"I'm so sorry, Fee!" one of her friends cried while she rubbed Fiona's back in manic circles. Fiona looked up from her handful of Kleenex for a second, her face thoughtful.

"I know! I'll name my first baby Carli. So I never forget her or our friendship." She broke down into sobs again.

"Oh, Fiona!"

"Fee, you're such an amazing friend."

"That's what Carli would have wanted."

"Wow," Mia said, catching up to me at the door where I stood with my mouth hanging open. "I wasn't sure I wanted to come to school today but I would have hated to miss this. Seriously, Fiona should charge admission." She was trying to keep things light but the laughter didn't make it to her red-rimmed eyes. I could see she was troubled. How could she not be? I slung an arm over her shoulder and led her inside.

If anything, the gossip was worse inside the school. I could hear snippets of conversations as Mia and I walked down the hallway.

"Did you hear they found her naked?"

"No way! Was she raped?"

"She had to be, right?"

"I heard she was completely gutted."

"What? That's disgusting!"

"Yeah, her druggie boyfriend did it."

"Freakin' Indians, man."

My face was burning. I could feel the heat seeping across my cheeks. Mia's face was as red as mine felt. She grabbed my hand and squeezed it.

"Have some respect!" I yelled into the crowd of kids. It was quiet for about five seconds. Just long enough for Mia to drag me away but not quite long enough that I didn't hear some Neanderthal football player mouth off to his friends.

"Now that sexy-ass squaw can yell at me any time she wants. Do you think she's that mouthy in bed?"

I was about to turn back around when I saw Jake talking to Ben at the end of the hall. My heart broke for Ben. He looked absolutely shattered. His eyes were watery. Jake had his hand on Ben's slumped shoulders, leaning down to talk to him.

"Poor Ben. Come on." Mia pulled me towards the guys and away from the football players. She walked up to Ben and hugged him tightly. Ben hugged her back, a tear sliding down his face. "I'm so sorry, Ben. I can't even imagine what you must be going through."

Jake and I looked at each other silently and then he turned back to Ben.

"Especially with all this shit." Jake gestured around the hall. I touched Ben's arm.

"I'm really sorry, Ben. Is there anything we can do?"

He smiled weakly at me. "Yeah. Get me out of here. I don't know what the hell I was thinking, coming to school today. But I was going crazy at home." We nodded at him. "They're all acting like I had something to do with it." He gestured down the crowded hallway.

"We know you didn't, buddy." Jake looked at him intently. "Come on. Let's go for a drive or something." He turned to Mia and me. "You guys want to come?"

"You bet." Mia picked up Ben's backpack and slung it over her shoulder with her own. I nodded and took her hand. Ben smiled sadly at me, then followed us out. We tried to shield him but the whispers intensified when we walked past. At least the parking lot was mostly empty now. The first bell had just rung so only the stragglers were left. The stragglers and two cops leaning against their squad car, laughing uproariously at something.

I was outraged but Ben looked devastated. The more they laughed, the more he seemed to shrink.

"They're not doing anything," he said, almost to himself. "They don't even care what happened to her." We had to lean in close to hear him as the cops brayed loudly again.

"Okay, that's it." I dropped Mia's hand and threw my purse to Jake, who caught it deftly. I stalked over to the cops.

"Hey. Hey! 5-0! Maybe you should drop the donuts and try to find out who killed our friend!"

"And maybe you should watch your mouth, little girl." One of the cops dragged his ass off the car and walked towards me.

"You haven't even started to hear my mouth yet," I told him. Jake and Mia arrived at my side and tried to usher me away. I looked at his name tag. "Why don't you do your job and catch the killer, Officer Dawson?"

"Killer?" He laughed and called over to his partner. "Did you hear that one? No killer, sweetheart. Just another depressed Indian girl taking a swan dive into the river." I felt like someone had slapped me.

"That's not true!" Ben screamed. "Carli would never kill herself! She had plans! *We* had plans. She didn't commit suicide. Someone did this to her and you're just sitting here laughing and letting whoever killed her get away with it."

Jake put an arm around Ben and led him away while Mia took my hand again and pulled me after them.

"Come on," she said. "They're not going to listen to us." I walked away with her, speechless as the cops laughed behind us.

CHAPTER 10
I'M FREE AS A BIRD NOW

He held the newspaper in his hands and read the headline.

"Local Girl Found in River Ruled a Suicide"

He hadn't meant for anyone to find her. He had weighted her body down but she must have come free of her shackles and washed down the river.

Somehow, despite the comedy of errors, he had gotten away with it. They thought she killed herself.

He stared at the picture of his little blackbird and laughed and laughed.

CHAPTER 11
SAYING GOODBYE

I hate to admit it, but that morning was one of the most awkward experiences of my life. We were all sad about Carli, but it was nothing compared to Ben's incredible grief.

It made no sense that anyone could see Ben and still believe on any level that he killed his girlfriend. He looked gutted. I immediately wished I hadn't thought of that word to describe Ben's emotional state. The echo of some random kid saying he heard Ben had gutted Carli was still too fresh in my mind.

I shook my head and looked at Jake. He was speaking in a low voice to Ben, clapping a hand on his back and trying so hard to make him feel better. How could he be so caring with Ben and so hateful about Matt and Dre? I looked at Mia, who was texting on her phone. She was always on her phone lately — and weirdly secretive about it.

"Who are you talking to?" I asked casually. She looked up at me. Was that guilt flashing in her eyes?

"No one."

I was slightly offended that she seemed to be hiding something from me. I was her best friend, after all. "Just something about homework. You know how I hate missing classes," she said. Well, that much was true. I felt bad. Maybe she was telling the truth.

Her phone vibrated and she checked it, a soft smile lighting up her face. Yeah, I wasn't buying it. She was definitely hiding something . . . or someone.

"Mia," I started, but Jake cut me off before I could challenge her on what were clearly lies.

"Hey, guys?" he called. "Ben wants to bring some flowers down to the river. For Carli."

"Okay!" Mia was quick to respond and step ahead of me to catch up to the guys. Whatever it was we needed to talk about would obviously have to wait until we were alone.

We all piled into Jake's Mazda 3 and drove away from the school. Mia and I slouched down in the back seat, just in case. No one ran after the car screaming "truant" at us, and we made it out of the parking lot safely. We stopped long enough to grab some flowers and headed down the river.

"Stop here," Ben told Jake. He pointed out a spot to park near the Midtown Bridge. It was eerie down here, even with the tourists and joggers and moms with their strollers on the Riverwalk. I knew Carli had gone missing here and had been found right down there in the water. Stupid as it sounds, it felt haunted. Not by a ghost, though. It felt as if something horrible had happened here.

We all got out of the car and headed down to the water together.

"This is where they found her," Ben whispered, almost to himself. He was staring at the river, watching it flow past. I couldn't help but imagine Carli here. I didn't believe for a second that she killed herself. But was she already dead when she went into the water? Was she afraid? Did she call out for

Ben? I shivered and Jake handed me his jacket. I nodded my thanks.

"There's no police tape or anything," I said. Why didn't they have the area taped off?

"They don't believe it's a crime scene," Ben replied. "They think she killed herself, so they're not investigating."

"Don't they have to look at all the options? What if they're wrong? Then we're walking all over the crime scene!" We all looked around, as if there might be a major clue under our feet. For all we knew, there was.

"Yeah, I know, Feather. But they wouldn't listen to me or to Carli's foster mom. We both told the cops she wouldn't kill herself. They just wanted to close the case and forget about her." He clutched the flowers tightly in his hand and looked over the water again. He stepped forward slowly and stopped at the river's edge. "I'm so sorry, baby," he said softly. We walked forward as a group and stood beside him. Mia took his free hand. "I'm sorry I wasn't there to protect you that night. I'm sorry no one will listen to me. I'm sorry you're gone. I wish . . ." He stopped and his breath hitched as he fought back tears. "I wish it had been me and not you." Mia squeezed his hand. "I still feel you with me. I won't ever forget you, Carli. I promise you that." He tossed the bouquet into the water and watched as it floated away on the current.

Mia stepped forward and held up the single rose she had bought.

"Rest in peace, Carli," she said. "We'll take care of Ben for you." She threw her rose into the river and stepped back.

Jake was next.

"I'll miss you, Carli. It's not the same at school without you. And my new lab partner is an idiot." We all smiled at that.

"You were one of a kind," he said and threw his rose.

My turn. I looked down at the rose in my hand and tried to think of something to say that would adequately express how sorry I was.

"Carli . . ." I stopped. A wave of grief for the bright, smiling girl I had grown up with washed over me. How were we supposed to make any sense of this? A perfectly healthy seventeen-year-old girl was dead. She was gone and she wasn't ever coming back. She'd never laugh at Mia's jokes or kiss Ben or bump into me as she walked down the hall at school with her face hidden by a library book. I couldn't wrap my head around it. She was just gone. I took a deep breath. God, why was this so hard? I tried again.

"Carli, I wish we had more time. Time to get to know each other again. Time to shop and watch movies and laugh together. But I'm grateful for the time I did spend with you. I'm glad you came to my birthday parties. Even though the balloons freaked you out." Ben and Mia laughed at that. "I'm glad we snuck out together to see that horror movie when we were twelve and I'm glad you stayed over that night because it scared the hell out of me. I'm sorry the police don't care what happened to you. But we do. We care. And . . . we'll keep fighting for the truth, Carli. We'll . . . we'll miss you." I threw my rose and watched it float gently down the river to join the other flowers. Ben hugged me tightly.

"Thank you." He hugged Mia next. Then Jake. "Thank you so much for coming with me. And for caring. She'd like that."

"Of course." Jake hugged Ben back. "Any time. Do you want to hang out at my place or something? My parents are both at work."

Ben shook his head.

"Nah. I think I'll try to get some sleep. I haven't been sleeping much . . ." He trailed off. Yeah. I could imagine.

"Mia?" Jake asked.

"It's almost lunchtime. I think I'll go catch my afternoon classes so I can work on my art project," she said.

"What about you, Feather?" He smiled at me, then lowered his voice. "We should probably talk."

"Yeah. I guess so. I don't really feel like going to math anyway," I told him.

"Okay. So we'll drop you guys off first then," he said to Ben and Mia. He smiled at me again. God, that smile that made the corners of his eyes crinkle always made my heart beat faster. So did the thought that we were going to be alone in his house for hours. I swallowed hard, trying to erase the memory of his hateful words about Matt and Dre from my head.

"Let's go, then," I said, looking at Mia, my cheeks burning as she winked at me. That girl knew me far too well.

CHAPTER 12
SECRETS

It was quiet in Jake's house. I was so used to his mother fluttering around the kitchen and his father yelling at the television while his twin brother and sister ran through the room and jumped on the sofa beside us repeatedly. I had been dating Jake for over a year and it was hard to find anywhere for us to be alone. And lately, well, let's just say we *really* wanted to be alone. I mean, it had been over a year. At the moment, I think we were both feeling emotional and needed to connect. We needed to feel something . . . to feel alive, I guess. Even if I was still kind of upset with him.

He opened the refrigerator and handed me a Diet Coke.

"Do you want anything else?" he asked. He rubbed his hand through his hair, a sure sign he was nervous.

"No. Just . . ." I trailed off, not meeting his eyes.

He sighed. "I know. I was an ass the other day. I was surprised and was trying to be funny and it didn't work."

"No. It didn't," I told him, softening a little.

"I'm sorry. I am. Matt and Dre are my friends."

"I know." I let him take my hand.

"So you forgive me?" He kissed my fingers. I was melting. I couldn't help it.

"I don't know." He kissed me. Softly. First on the lips. Then on the cheek. And on my neck, nibbling my collarbone. God, he was killing me. I desperately tried to hang onto my outrage.

"Are you sure you don't want anything else?" he asked, nuzzling into my throat, his hand moving up my rib cage. I shivered. Ah, hell. I could be mad later. I decided to go with it.

"Well, I'd like to see your room," I told him, boldly. We weren't allowed to hang out in his room usually. He blushed, the pink rising from his cheeks and turning the tips of his ears red. He was adorable. I took his hand and led him to his bedroom.

"Should we leave the door open?" he asked. I looked at him, surprised. Then I saw him smile mischievously. I slapped his arm. He grabbed my hand and pulled me against him, wrapping his arms around me. "Kinda weird being alone for once," he said, kissing my neck.

"Mm-hmm . . ." He was making it difficult to concentrate on anything other than what he was doing. I wrapped my arms around his neck and kissed him, hard, as his hand moved to my waist and under my shirt. "What time will your parents be home?" "Not until six," he murmured. He pulled away from me and looked into my eyes. "Feather . . . we don't have to . . ." He blushed again.

"I know!" I was suddenly blushing too. "But I want to. I don't want to wait anymore." I looked down at my hands. "I feel like life is so short. What if something happened to you? Or to me? I don't want to regret anything. I don't want to miss out on anything."

"I know." He kissed me again. He buried his fingers in my hair, wrapping it around his hands then pulling — violently. I gasped in surprise at the sudden pain as my neck was exposed. I felt a jolt of fear.

"Jake . . . ?" My voice wavered. He held my hair tightly, then leaned down and bit my neck. "Ouch!" I tried to push him away but he pinned my hands together and bit harder. "Stop, Jake!" The bite turned into a kiss. As if he had meant it to be a kiss all along. He pulled me back onto the bed. Breathing harder. Whispering my name. Telling me that he loved me.

I tried to shake off a feeling that was too close to fear and focus on being in the moment. I struggled to picture myself as a sexy, alluring woman instead of the nervous girl who was feeling uneasy around her boyfriend. I was failing miserably until he kissed his way down my neck, across my collarbone and down the middle of my chest. When he reached the curve of my stomach, I was completely lost in him.

× × ×

I pulled on my clothes afterwards, suddenly shy. I was sore in places I barely knew existed. Jake reached out and rubbed my back.

"Are you okay?" he asked.

I nodded, not meeting his eyes. I wasn't sure what to feel. If I was being honest, I hadn't enjoyed it. The truth was it hadn't been what I expected. Jake's behaviour hadn't been what I expected. He hadn't hurt me exactly. And I had been more than willing. But it wasn't gentle and loving like I had expected. I couldn't put my finger on it, but there was something not quite right. Maybe it was because I was still upset with him. That must be it, I told myself.

"So stay," he pulled at my hand. I jerked it away.

"I . . . um . . . I should get out of here before your parents get home. And . . . uh . . . I should get home and help Kiowa with dinner." I couldn't meet his eyes. His parents really would be home any minute, so it was easy to get out the door quickly after I called Mia to come and get me. He left me at the door with a far gentler kiss than any he had given me in his bed. I shook my head as I got into the car and closed the door behind me. I could still feel his hands roughly pulling my head backwards. I closed my eyes, willing myself to focus on the sweet kiss he had given me at the door. *That* was my Jake.

"Ahem." Mia cleared her throat dramatically . "So . . . how was it?" She had waited until she turned off Jake's street to start interrogating me. Frankly, I couldn't believe she had held out as long as she did.

"I don't know," I answered. "It was . . . okay."

"Just okay?" she asked.

"I mean . . . oh my God, this is so embarrassing!"

"Oh please. I told you everything last summer when I slept with that guy at art camp," she reminded me.

"More than I needed to know, quite frankly," I told her.

"Yeah, yeah. So? Tell me!"

"Okay. Well, it wasn't what I imagined. I thought it would be more like *Twilight*. It kinda hurt actually. And I think it was more fun for him than it was for me," I confessed, purposely avoiding telling her how rough he had been with me. I didn't know what to think and I couldn't handle her questions right now.

"Well, obviously." She snickered. "It'll take awhile for you to really enjoy it."

"Wait, how do you know that?" As far as I knew, the art camp guy was the only boy she had slept with. I thought about those secretive texts she had been getting. "Something you're not telling me?" I asked her mildly. Her secrecy was starting to wear thin, but I couldn't force anything out of her.

"No. But I do read, Feather. And talk to people," she replied. "And I watch HBO."

"It's not like the movies," I admitted. She nodded knowingly. "I'm definitely glad we waited until we were ready. And I'm glad my first time was with someone I love. I don't know. I guess that sounds stupid."

"No it doesn't," she said. "To be honest, I wish I had waited. Tom was nice and all but I didn't really care about him. I wish it had been with someone I did care about. You're lucky, Feather."

"I guess." I shrugged. "But Mia? I feel like you and I haven't really talked lately."

"What do you mean?" she asked. "We're talking right now."

I rolled my eyes.

"No, I mean . . . we haven't really caught up lately. You obviously know what's new with me. But what have you been up to?" It was the perfect opening for her to tell me what she'd been hiding. She didn't take it.

"Nothing. You know me. School, home, nothing exciting."

I sighed. "Have you talked to your mom yet?"

"I haven't even seen her for more than five minutes at a time. Just as she passes through the house on her way out," she said.

"Mia, you have to talk to her."

"I know, Feather! I will! Let me tell her in my own time, okay? This isn't easy for me. My mom isn't like yours." She rubbed angrily at her eyes. She always hated to cry and I knew I had pushed her as far as she'd let me.

"I'm sorry. But if you need anything or if I can help . . ." I trailed off as she pulled into my driveway. "Do you want to stay for dinner?" I saw her glance at Kiowa's car.

"Nah. I don't want to intrude. Lots of homework and stuff," she said. It felt as if she was blowing me off.

"Yeah. Me too." We had never been awkward with each other before and I had no idea how to fix it. "I'm here for you, you know. You can talk to me if something is going on."

"Nothing is going on!" She was completely exasperated now. She looked at me and her expression softened. "I'm just busy."

I nodded, not believing her for a second.

CHAPTER 13
SAFETY IN NUMBERS

I woke up the next morning to a deluge of rain slamming against my bedroom window. I love the sound of rain but I had always hated driving in it, so I was debating whether to be happy about the rain or curse it.

I stretched, feeling a bite of pain in my lower body. Smiling, I sat up and threw my legs over the side of the bed. I ached all over, as if I had worked out. I guess I had, in a way. I wondered idly if anyone would be able to tell. Did I look any different now? I definitely felt different. I stretched once more and got out of bed. I guess I'd find out soon enough. I could hear my mom rattling around in the kitchen. I looked into the mirror and gasped, the smile sliding off my face. There was a purple, almost black, bruise colouring the base of my neck where Jake had bitten me. If I had been fooling myself that this was a love bite, the fact that I could see where his teeth broke the skin would have quickly cured me of that illusion. It looked like a dog had attacked me. Luckily, my shirt covered it, but as I stared at the spot where his teeth had torn into my skin, I shivered. What kind of person would do that? Who gets off on hurting his partner like that? I pushed a sudden thought of Carli out of my head. I pulled the collar of my shirt up and headed into the kitchen.

"Hey, honey. Do you want eggs?" My mom kissed me on the cheek and handed me a glass of orange juice. I sipped from it, looking at her from under my eyelashes.

"No. I'll just make some toast. Thanks." I reached for the bread and slid two slices into the toaster. My mom handed me the peanut butter. "Thanks, Mom." She hugged me and grabbed her purse off the kitchen table.

"Okay, I'm going to be late if I don't get out of here right now. Your brother is still sleeping."

"No I'm not." Kiowa walked into the kitchen, yawning widely.

"Okay then, he's not. Have a good day, you two."

She was gone before I could reply and I called out "You too!" to an empty doorway. I shrugged.

"Smooth." Kiowa poured himself a cup of coffee. He squinted at me. "Did you change your hair or something?" Oh God. My brother's the one who notices something's different about me?

"Ummm . . . no?" He studied me again. "New T-shirt," I told him. He nodded at me and poured cream into his coffee mug. "When are you going back to school?" I asked. "Isn't the next term starting??"

"Nope." he asked me, sticking his head into the refrigerator and coming back out with a package of corned beef. Damn. I had been so distracted lately that I'd been ignoring my brother after not seeing him for weeks.

"Right. Sorry. It's just been a crazy week," I told him.

"Yeah, I know. It's okay. I get it." He opened the package of meat and began pulling it out with a fork and piling it on a piece of bread.

"Is that all you're having?" I asked him.

"No, dork. I'm making a Reuben," he said, pulling a jar of sauerkraut towards him. I wrinkled my nose and took a bite of toast.

"It's 8:30 in the morning!"

He smiled at me and shrugged. "I was up all night studying." He slathered another piece of bread with Russian dressing. "Aren't you going to be late picking up Mia?" he asked, nodding at the clock.

"Damn it! Yeah." I grabbed my keys off the counter and slung my backpack over my shoulder. "Get some sleep," I told him. He nodded and waved bye to me with his fork.

I drove to Mia's with the windshield wipers going full blast. I turned onto her street and pulled into her driveway, honking as I shifted into park. No way was I going out into this monsoon unless I absolutely had to. I saw the door open and Mia come flying down the stairs, the hood of her raincoat shielding her face. She pulled open the car door and threw herself into the passenger seat.

"Holy shit!" she said, pushing her hood away from her face. "I think it might be time to build a freakin' ark."

"Language," I laughed.

"Sorry. But seriously. This is insane. I keep expecting the wicked witch to fly past on a bicycle."

"That was a tornado, not a rainstorm," I told her. She looked thoughtful for a second.

"Shit. You're right."

"Since when do you swear like a sailor?" I asked.

"Since I started watching cable." She laughed. "So I talked to Matt last night. He's coming back to school today."

"Really? That's great. Is Dre back today too?" I asked.

"He didn't say. Listen, Feather, I really want to be supportive." She paused and then blurted out the rest. "Is Jake going to be a dick with Matt?"

"No! We talked about it. He said he was just making a joke because he was uncomfortable and didn't know what to say."

"I hope you're right. You're cool with supporting Matt?" she asked.

"I'm in. I like Matt and what happened to him sucked," I told her, turning into the school parking lot. I was happy to change the subject. "You ready?" I asked, putting my hood up and holding the door handle.

"Let's do it," she screamed. We threw ourselves out of the car at the same time and ran into the school, laughing as the rain pelted us furiously.

"That was insane!" I giggled.

"Remember when we used to dance in the rain when we were kids?" Mia asked, unzipping her jacket.

"Of course." I smiled and then spotted Matt at the other end of the hallway. I elbowed Mia. "There's Matt." She looked down the hall and frowned. Matt was walking towards us with his head down and his shoulders slumped. Kids were whispering and pointing, and we could hear the snorts of laughter from here. "Fag," someone stage whispered to a round of snickers.

"Ah hell," Mia groaned. "Come on." She grabbed my hand and pulled me down the hallway. "Matt!" she called out. "Hey, Matt!"

He looked up cautiously and relief washed over his face when he spotted us waving and smiling at him like a couple of lunatics. His pace picked up until he was standing in front of us. I leaned in and gave him a big hug. I felt him let out a long, shuddering breath as he hugged me back.

"Hey, Feather," he said, leaning back and looking down at me. "I was starting to wonder if anyone was going to talk to me."

"Well, we will. You've got us to walk down the hall with and to sit with at lunch too. Whatever you need, okay?" He nodded, and then turned to hug Mia.

"Is Dre back today too?" she asked him.

He shook his head sadly.

"No. His parents decided they don't want a gay son. They're sending him to some kind of anti-gay military school."

I looked at him, shocked.

"That's awful. Do they really think military school is going to make him straight?"

He raised his eyebrows at me.

"Considering it's an all-boys school, I'm kinda guessing it'll have the opposite effect. I honestly don't know what they're thinking."

"How are your parents? Are they cool?" Mia asked.

"Yeah, they're actually pretty awesome." Matt smiled. "I came out to them about a year ago and they told me they love me no matter what."

"I didn't know you came out last year," I said, grabbing his hand and starting towards our period one English class.

"Just to my family," he said. "And they've been amazing. They really have. Not like all of my so-called friends." He gestured around the hallway where people were still whispering about him. Matt was one of the most popular guys at school. At least he was until he got caught in his car with Dre.

"We're still your friends and you can hang out with us any time," Mia told him.

"Definitely," I added.

"Thanks, guys. I mean it. I don't know if I would have gotten through the morning without a friendly face."

Jake sauntered over and kissed me on the cheek. I mentally stopped myself from pulling away from him. He rubbed my shoulder before noticing Matt was standing with us.

"Oh. Hey, Matt." He shifted awkwardly from foot to foot.

"Hey, Jake." Matt smiled cautiously.

"So . . . uh. Where's Dre?" Jake pulled at the collar of his T-shirt, visibly beginning to sweat.

"He transferred to another school."

"Oh. For people who want to kill themselves?" Jake asked.

"Jake!" I smacked his arm.

"What? I heard he was suicidal," he said.

"Will you just stop talking?" I slapped his arm harder.

"It's fine, Feather." Matt smiled weakly. I saw him glance over at a group of kids whispering loudly and laughing as they pointed at Matt. He blushed brightly.

"Mind your business!" Mia growled at them.

"Thanks, Mia." Matt smiled.

"No problem. I'll meet you guys after class." She slipped into the class next to ours.

Jake stopped awkwardly outside my class.

"So . . . see you later." He turned and walked away. I watched him stop to talk to Ben at his locker before heading off. I didn't know what they were saying but Jake didn't look happy. He looked like he was confronting Ben about something. By the time he stalked away, Ben looked upset too. I couldn't help but feel that Ben got lucky in a weird kind of way. Everyone was talking about Matt and Dre. They had forgotten all about blaming Ben for Carli's death.

We got through the rest of the day uneventfully. Mia and I bracketed Matt everywhere he went, and Jake met us after every class, looking uncomfortable every time Matt looked his way. I had no idea how he kept getting out of class early enough to meet us, but he was there waiting, without fail after every single bell. Sometimes he was leaning against the wall with Ben beside him, their argument apparently forgotten. Sometimes he was alone. But after every class, there he was. Was he keeping an eye on me?

CHAPTER 14
THE FIRST 48 HOURS

Aside from the odd homophobic comment called out by meatheads, people were quickly losing interest. Matt was smiling and holding his head significantly higher than he had that morning. Even Ben had a smile on his face. Circle of life, I thought to myself.

The five of us were all laughing as we walked past the office and out the front doors of the school. Then Ben's smile died on his face.

The same two police officers were back and hanging around outside the school, but they weren't leaning against their squad car or eating donuts this time. Today, they were wrestling with a hysterical woman on the front stairs. One had both arms wrapped around her waist and was trying to throw her to the ground while the other had one hand gripped on her arm so tightly, his knuckles were white. His other hand was holding a Taser, which he was waving at the screaming woman. Tears were running down her face and she was sobbing as if her heart was broken.

"Robin!" Ben yelled, breaking away from us and running down the stairs. "Get away! Leave her alone!" He reached the woman before any of us even registered what was happening.

"Ben!" Mia screamed and practically shoved me down the stairs as she rushed towards him. We all followed, trying to reach Ben before he punched one of the cops. A crowd was gathering, shooting video with their cell phones and watching from a safe distance.

"Get off her!" Ben shouted, grabbing one of the cops by the arm. Unfortunately, not the one with the Taser. Taser cop pointed his weapon at Ben just as we reached him.

"Stop!" I screamed, jumping in front of Ben. I admit, I didn't really think that one through. The last thing I wanted was to be hit by a Taser, but there I was, in front of Ben, blocking the cop's shot.

Jake pulled Ben away from the cop and both men let go of the crying woman — Robin — and she slumped down onto the stairs.

"I'm okay," Ben told Jake. He knelt down beside the woman and touched her shoulder. "Robin? What are you doing here?" The woman slumped into Ben's arms, crying uncontrollably.

"I came to talk to you," she sobbed. "They told me I had to leave and called the police."

"Get her out of here before I arrest her!" one of the cops said.

"For what?" I asked him. She didn't look like much of a threat.

"Disturbing the peace? Assaulting a police officer?" he replied, straightening his uniform.

"From what I could see, you were assaulting her! We all saw it." Jake, Matt and Mia nodded. "Ben, what can we do? Should I call someone?"

"No. It's okay. This is Robin, Carli's foster mom." He rubbed her back. Her sobs started to taper off and she looked up at him, her face red and tear-stained.

"Ben, they won't listen to me! I told them Carli wouldn't kill herself."

"I know she wouldn't, Robin. I told them the same thing." We hung back, unsure what to do.

"I saw her, Ben. I had to go and identify her." She choked on a sob. Ben looked shocked.

"I didn't know, Robin. I'm so sorry."

"She had bruises on her neck. Like someone had choked her. Her hands were all cut up, like she was trying to fight off someone. She didn't kill herself. I know she didn't. Someone did that to her!" She was looking at him, begging him to hear her.

"Wait . . . what? She had injuries? Why didn't they do an autopsy?" Ben asked. She just shook her head.

"I don't know," she said helplessly. "They said she had been in the river too long to tell when she had been injured. I told them the marks weren't there when she left the house but they said it could have happened any time before she died. Why won't they listen? Someone killed her and I didn't protect her." She buried her face in Ben's shoulder and he stared up at us, shock written on his face.

I looked at the cops standing nearby. "Why didn't they do an autopsy?" I asked.

"I assume because the coroner didn't think they needed to." He shrugged carelessly but his partner looked extremely uncomfortable.

"But if she had injuries? Why wouldn't they check?" I'd watched enough TV crime shows to know it was important they start looking for a killer right away. Once the evidence was gone, they wouldn't have a chance of finding out who had done this to Carli.

"I don't know, kid. I'm not the coroner, okay?" The cop strolled over to his car and got in. He honked for his partner, who stood with his hat in his hands.

"I'm sorry for your loss," he mumbled before walking to the car.

"Ben, we should take her home," Jake told him. He helped Ben get Robin to her feet and lead her to his car.

I looked around at the kids sending videos to their friends, as if this were entertainment. I shook my head and walked to my car, followed by a speechless Mia and Matt. The kids were already whispering behind us.

"I *knew* her boyfriend killed her!"

"The cops have to arrest him now."

I heard the gossip escalating until I closed my car door and shut out the voices.

CHAPTER 15
BYE-BYE BLACKBIRD

He stared at the empty room, scrubbed clean and tangy with the sharp smell of bleach. His mother's old records echoed in here when it was empty. They echoed around him now.

He hated being alone. He was only truly happy when he had someone there with him.

Someone to complete him.

Until she disappointed him.

They always disappointed him.

And when he was disappointed, it was time to take out the trash.

So to speak.

He saw a long black hair stuck in a crack in the wall and plucked it out. He studied it for a second and then dropped it into the garbage bag at his feet before hitting the light switch and plunging his special room into complete darkness.

CHAPTER 16
COMING CLEAN

When we dropped Matt off at his house on the way to Mia's, he hugged us both tightly. I felt the air whoosh out of me as he squeezed me.

"I couldn't have gotten through this day without you guys. It means a lot that you stood by me."

"We're not going anywhere," Mia told him, hugging him back. He walked up to his front door with his head up and a smile on his face. He was far from the slump-shouldered, dejected guy who had walked the school hallway this morning. It was nice to see and I was proud to have helped in some small way. As we pulled out of the driveway, Matt's mom opened the door and gave him a huge hug before they went into the house.

"I'm so glad his family is cool with him," I told Mia. She nodded in response and glanced down at her phone.

"Yeah. But I'm not sure Jake is," she said.

"What do you mean? He's trying, Mia."

"Stop making excuses for him! It's pretty clear that he's not all right with Matt being gay."

"You saw him today," I insisted. "He met us after every class! He's making an effort, unlike half the Neanderthals at our school." My heart was pounding.

"Okay, okay. I'm sorry. Maybe I'm wrong."

"You are," I told her even though I knew deep down that she wasn't. I didn't even know why I was defending him.

I pulled into Mia's driveway behind Leonard's black pick-up truck. He had no job and no money of his own but he sure loved putting cash into his truck. Big monster tires and a custom paint job. All paid for by Mia's mom, of course. I felt rather than heard Mia's intake of breath beside me. I looked at her quizzically. We may be butting heads about Jake but she was still my best friend.

"You okay?" I asked.

She sighed and slumped down in her seat. "Yeah. It's just . . . he told me he'd be out tonight."

"He's still hassling you?" I already knew the answer before she nodded. She hadn't invited me over as much as usual. I figured it was because he was home. It appears I was right.

"Yeah." She left it at that and made no move to get out of the car. I touched her arm so she'd look at me.

"Maybe you should stay at my place for a couple of days," I told her.

She shook her head. "No, it's fine. Are you coming in for a bit?"

Mia reached for the door handle. I wasn't going to leave her alone with her scumbag stepfather any longer than I had to. "Yeah, of course!" She looked at me with a funny expression. "I mean, we do have math homework."

She nodded again. "Just . . . nothing." She frowned as she got out of the car and grabbed her bag from the back seat. I grabbed my own backpack and followed behind her. It bothered me that her posture looked a lot like Matt's had looked that morning. It was as if she was on her way to an execution.

I started to think things had become even worse for her at home. Considering how bad they were in the first place . . . I had Matt's back and I definitely had Mia's back too.

Leonard was waiting at the door when we walked in, a lecherous smirk on his face.

"Well, hello lovely ladies," he bowed to us. It was almost comical, him in his stained wife-beater shirt, trying to be classy.

Mia skirted around him, deftly avoiding any contact. "I thought you were going out," she muttered in his general direction.

He scratched his crotch absentmindedly and looked at Mia's chest. "Your mom is coming home early. I thought we could have a family dinner tonight." He looked pointedly at me.

"I'll be on my way when she gets here then," I said, crossing my arms over my chest.

"I hope you don't expect me to make dinner," Mia told him.

"Nope, I've got it covered." He nodded towards the stove. "Meatloaf, mashed potatoes and green beans."

Mia walked over to the stove and lifted the lid off one of the pots. Before she could turn around or walk away, Leonard was behind her, pressing his body into hers and pretending to reach for something above her head.

"Hey!" Mia yelled, pinned against the stove.

"Get off her!" I grabbed Leonard's arm and pulled him backwards. He turned and looked at me, shock written all over his face. His fist was up in an instant, threatening to come down on my face. He might have done it if the front door hadn't opened at that moment. Mia's mother called out a greeting.

"I'm home!" she sang out, her heels clicking down the hallway towards us. Leonard lowered his hand and Mia grabbed mine. She dragged me around him and out of the kitchen.

"Hi, Mom," she called over her shoulder as she pulled me into her bedroom and firmly closed the door behind us. She slid the lock closed and turned, falling onto the bed with a sigh.

"Mia, what the hell was that?"

"Do not start with me, Feather. I know, okay? I need to tell my mother. And she's actually home tonight," she told me. "I know."

"So you'll talk to her?" I asked.

"Sure, Feather. Should I talk to her before or after she sleeps with Leonard while he pretends that she's me? Yeah, he actually told me he does that."

"Oh my God, Mia. Has this been happening with him every night?" I gestured towards the door, and then noticed for the first time that it was hanging crookedly. The frame looked as if someone had kicked it in. "Mia," I breathed, looking at her as she refused to meet my eyes. "What the hell happened here?"

"Nothing."

"Mia! Tell me the truth for once!" She looked at me, suddenly furious.

"Fine. What do you want to hear, Feather?"

"The truth!" I told her angrily.

"The truth? Okay. Like how he got drunk and didn't like that I locked him out so he kicked in the door?"

"No," I breathed.

"Yes. How he climbed onto my bed and put his hands all over me? How he tried to pin me down and told me he knew I wanted it while he undid his pants?"

"Oh my God, Mia. He raped you?" I asked.

"No, Feather. He didn't. Because Carli taught me to keep this close." She slid a knife from under her pillow and held it up. "I held this against his crotch and told him I'd cut it off before I let him have sex with me. And you know what he did?" I shook my head wordlessly. "He laughed. He did his pants back up and laughed at me."

"Why didn't you tell me?" I asked, wiping tears from my eyes. "You could have stayed with me."

Mia stopped and looked at me before sighing.

"I've been staying at the rec centre a lot." She glanced over at me through her hair. "And hanging out down by the river."

"Mia!" I sputtered. "Why? You know you can stay with me any time! Why would you go down there? Carli went missing somewhere along the Riverwalk!"

"I didn't stay with you in your perfect house with your perfect mother because I didn't want yet another lecture about why I wasn't talking to my own mother!" she blurted out. I felt the colour drain out of my face.

"Mia . . ." My mouth opened and closed like a fish out of water. "I'm sorry. I didn't mean to . . ." I trailed off. "I had no idea you were so upset with me. That's why you've been acting so secretive."

"Yeah, well . . ." she said, not meeting my eyes. She didn't look angry. She looked guilty.

"Mia, we've been friends since we were kids. I'm sorry if I lectured you. I worry about you. You can always stay with me if you need to. And if you're pissed off at me, you can relegate me to Kiowa's disgusting room." She smiled at that. "I mean it, Mia. I will try not to push, but if I do, it's because you're like a sister to me and I don't want anything bad to happen to you."

"I know," she said. "But you have to let me handle it in my own time, okay? You have to trust me, Feather."

I nodded.

"I trust you, Mia. Do you want to stay with me tonight? I can't sleep in Kiowa's room, because he's home right now, but the basement couch pulls out." She threw a pillow at my head.

"No, I'm going to stay home and eat some amazing meatloaf because believe it or not, the bastard can cook and I'm starving." I shook my head and laughed. "And I need to talk to my mom."

I looked over her head, nodding sagely. "Yeah, that's a good idea. If you want to talk to her."

Mia smacked me on the arm. "Oh shut up." There was a knock on the door and Mia's mom stuck her head in.

"Dinner's ready, Mia. Are you staying for dinner, Feather? Len made his world famous meatloaf." She smiled at me and I felt a jolt of sadness for her. She could be such a sweet woman sometimes. And she worked her ass off to support her deadbeat husband who, apparently unknown to her, couldn't keep his hands off her daughter.

"I can't tonight. I'm sorry. Kiowa's home for a couple of weeks and I promised we would eat together as a family."

"Some other time then. Mia, wash up and come to the table." She disappeared and I stood up and grabbed my bag.

"Call me later, okay?" I leaned over and gave her a hug.

"I will," she told me, hugging me hard. "Come on. I'll walk you out." She looped her arm through mine and smiled. "I'm actually feeling pretty good about talking to my mom," she told me. "She seems to be in a decent mood tonight."

"I think it'll help," I told her.

"Me too."

I left with the smell of Leonard's meatloaf wafting around me.

CHAPTER 17
A CRY IN THE NIGHT

The ringing of my cell phone woke me up from a dead sleep around midnight. I rolled over to reach for it and got tangled in the sheets, nearly sending myself crashing onto the floor. I spit a mouthful of hair out and grabbed the phone off my night table. I fumbled to answer it with my eyes still firmly shut.

"'Lo?" I muttered, falling back against my pillows. Silence. Then a sob. I sat up, my blood running cold. "Hello?" I was wide awake now. "Who is this?" More crying.

I barely registered the sound of the front door closing, and then remembered Kiowa was home.

"Feather?" A heartbreaking voice I only barely recognized as being Mia's.

"Mia? What is it? Did he do something to you?" I was on my feet in an instant, pacing the room.

"Nnnnooo." I had never heard her like this. Her breath hitched as she tried to stop crying. "She didn't believe me, Feather."

"She didn't . . . what?" I felt ice cold. This was my fault. I pushed Mia into telling her mom about Leonard. My hands were shaking so hard I nearly dropped my phone. "How could she not believe you?" I asked.

"He told her I was lying! He said I was always throwing myself at him when she wasn't home and he was too embarrassed to tell her."

"Oh my God, Mia. And she believed him?" I couldn't wrap my head around this. She was Mia's mom! And Leonard was disgusting. How could she not believe her own daughter?

"Yyyeeessss," Mia wailed.

"But you're her daughter!" I was outraged.

"She doesn't care! She said he was her husband and a good relationship is based on trust. She believed he was telling the truth."

"But why would you lie about something like that?" I asked her.

"She said maybe it was because she wasn't giving me enough attention and I wanted to get back at her for neglecting me. Or maybe I was jealous of their relationship."

"I can't believe this. I'm so sorry. I'll talk to her," I promised. "I'll tell her what I saw."

"It won't make a difference. I told you this was a bad idea. I told you I couldn't talk to her! If I don't apologize to Leonard for lying about him, I have to leave."

"Then you can stay here! I'll come and get you right now." I grabbed a hoodie off the back of my bedroom door and started to pull it on, holding the phone against my ear with my shoulder.

"No, it's okay, Feather," she replied quickly. Too quickly.

"What? Why? I can be there in fifteen minutes, Mia. Maybe less. You can't stay there."

"I know that!" she said. "Why are you still pushing me? I already have someone picking me up, okay? I'm going down to the rec centre for the night."

"Wouldn't you rather be here than at the rec centre with a bunch of strangers? And it's already midnight!" I couldn't imagine why she'd want to be at the centre on a cot when I'd happily let her sleep in my bed.

"I need some time to think things over, Feather," she said.

"What do you mean? What do you have to think over?" I asked, confused.

"I need to figure out where I'm going to go and what I'm going to do. I can't live with them anymore, obviously."

"So come here and think about it!" I insisted.

"No. I can't. Not tonight. It's late and Michael can help me figure things out. "

I had met Michael once or twice. He was cool for a guy who ran a rec centre. But he wasn't her best friend.

"Mia, I really think you should come here tonight. Go see Michael tomorrow," I pleaded.

"I just need to lie low for a couple of days."

"What are you not telling me, Mia?" I asked.

She sighed. "We'll talk tomorrow, okay? I know we need to talk. I want to tell you everything. Just not tonight. Try to understand."

I didn't understand. I'd never been in her position so I didn't really get it. But obviously the last thing she needed was another lecture from me.

"If that's what you want, I'll try to understand. Just call me in the morning, all right?"

"I will. I promise. Thanks."

"And if you need anything, just ask," I told her. "I'll leave my phone on all night, just in case you change your mind."

"Thanks, Feather. Love you," she said.

"Love you back."

I hung up and sat down on my bed. I couldn't help but think I should have insisted on picking her up. I knew she was upset with me. She had obviously been keeping secrets from me, but we had been friends a long time. We always managed to work things out. I pulled off my hoodie and got back into bed.

I was nearly asleep before it occurred to me I wasn't the first person she had called tonight. Someone else was picking her up and I hadn't even asked who. I stared up at the ceiling in the dark and wondered who had taken my place in my best friend's life.

× × ×

"She hasn't called yet?" Jake asked during our lunch break together.

"No. And she's not answering my calls or texts," I told him, obsessively texting Mia once more.

Mia, text me back right now. You're freaking me out! Mia hadn't shown up at school and her radio silence was scaring the hell out of me.

Where are you? I typed.

"So what did she say last night? Was she planning on coming to school?"

"I don't know," I admitted. "She didn't say anything about skipping but she was really upset. Maybe she decided to blow it off. But that doesn't explain why she isn't answering," I told him.

"You said she was upset when she left home. Maybe she forgot to grab her charger and her phone died," he said, logically. Logical except for one thing.

"But it's still ringing, Jake."

"Maybe she left it somewhere by mistake."

"There's no way, Jake. She never goes anywhere without her phone. She saved her money to get a waterproof case so she could take it with her in the shower. There's no possible way she forgot it somewhere. Something's wrong."

He studied my face. "Maybe someone stole it?" he ventured.

"Maybe . . ." I looked down at the silent-as-a-tomb phone in my hands and sighed. "But I really don't think so, Jake."

CHAPTER 18
O BLACKBIRD! SING ME SOMETHING WELL

He turned her phone over and over in his hands, rubbing his fingers over the smooth pink rubber case.

He stared intently at the screensaver. Two beautiful girls looked back at him, smiles lighting up their perfect, young faces.

"You're happy to see me, aren't you?" he cooed at them.

The phone chirped suddenly in his hands.

"Feather," he read, touching the photo that flashed on the screen. Now he knew her name.

CHAPTER 19
NUCLEAR FAMILY

By the time the last bell rang at 3:15, I was worried sick and checking my phone obsessively for any word from Mia. Although her phone was still ringing when I called it, she hadn't replied to any of my texts or picked up any of my calls. I had asked around and no one else had heard from her today either. It was as if she had dropped off the face of the earth.

Jake was waiting outside of my class. He was typing on his phone, his handsome face clouded by a frown.

"Who are you texting?" I asked him, standing on my toes to kiss his cheek. He looked at me, his features softening.

"I wasn't texting," he said. "I was checking to see if Mia posted anything on Instagram today."

I looked at him, completely surprised. Surprised he thought of checking Instagram and it hadn't occurred to me to do the same.

"That's a great idea. Has she posted anything?"

He shook his head.

"Nothing since yesterday."

I sighed and looked down at my phone for the millionth time. Nothing.

"Now what?" Jake asked, rubbing my back in slow circles. His mini massages usually relaxed me into a puddle but not today.

"I think we should go by her house," I told him. "Maybe she went back there? Or maybe they know what's going on at least."

"Good idea." Jake nodded. "I'll drive." He led me outside to his car and opened the door for me.

We were quiet on the ride to Mia's house. Jake fiddled with the radio for awhile before turning it off. He held my hand and smiled at me, kissing my fingers.

"She probably just needs some time alone. I'm sure she's okay, Feather."

"Are you?" I asked him. Because I wasn't sure. The longer she went without calling me, the less sure I became. Maybe we needed some backup. "Should we get Ben or Matt to come?"

When I mentioned Matt's name, I watched Jake's face change before he had a chance to paste on a smile. But I recognized the expression before it disappeared. It was distaste.

"Nah," he said. I tried to ignore the uneasy feeling I had about his reaction but it bothered me. I pushed it down. Not dismissing it — just saving that conversation for a better time. We needed to focus on finding Mia.

The drive to her house seemed to take forever. Maybe because I was dreading talking to Leonard. What was I supposed to say? Should I tell him what a douche bag he was for lying to Mia's mom? Slap him in the face? Both seemed like legitimate options. We pulled into the driveway behind Leonard's pickup truck, and to my shock, Mia's mother's car. I looked over at Jake.

"Her mom's here too."

"That's a good thing, right? She'd know more about Mia than her stepdad would."

"Yeah, maybe. It's weird. She's never home." I didn't wait for him to open the door for me this time. I got out of the car and stared up at the house, trying to figure out what to say to these awful people.

"Let's go talk to them." Jake held out his hand to me. I looked at him for a second, trying to get my nerves under control. I took his hand and squeezed it tightly. Uneasy as I was about him lately, I needed his support desperately.

"Let's do this," I agreed.

I had been to Mia's house hundreds of times. It was like a second home to me growing up. I barely remembered her father. Mia reminisced about him like he was a saint and life was perfect before he died, but I remembered being woken up by angry voices at her house too many times to believe her. I remembered the way he smelled when he said good night to us. Like stale cigarettes and alcohol. And I remembered the bruises on her mother's arms that she hid with sweaters even when it was hot outside. But I also remembered her baking cookies with us and taking us to movies. I remembered a mother who loved her daughter.

After her husband died, Mia's mom changed. She bleached her hair and wore too much makeup. She stayed out late and brought men home. Then she married Leonard and turned into someone I barely recognized. She hadn't had time for her daughter since she lost her husband and started searching single-mindedly for his replacement. Her life revolved around taking care of Leonard, a deadbeat in the truest sense of the word. But how could she ignore her own daughter's claim of abuse and throw her out of her home in the middle of the night? I just didn't get it. I was incredibly nervous to see her now.

I rang the doorbell and a tinkly version of "Ode to Joy" echoed faintly inside the joyless house. I heard shuffling footsteps and a grunt as Leonard unlocked the door. He pushed it open until it was stopped by the safety chain, then he peered blearily though the crack.

"Yeah?" he grunted, scratching at his unshaven chin.

"Is Mia here?" I asked.

"Who're you?" he asked. Huh?

"Are you serious? We've met hundreds of times. I was here yesterday! I'm her best friend." Was he high? I looked at Jake incredulously. He shook his head in disbelief and shrugged.

"Oh right. I didn't recognize you. Heather, right?" Oh my God. I caught the strong smell of marijuana drifting out of the house behind him.

"FEA-THER," I said, enunciating each syllable and rolling my eyes.

"Feather! Right. What do you want?" I gritted my teeth and dug my nails into my palms to keep from smacking him.

"Mia. Is she here?"

"No. Haven't seen her. Have you?"

"Obviously not, Leonard. Can I talk to Joyce, please?" I hoped her mom was less intoxicated. She was bound to be lucid enough to recognize me at least.

"Yeah, okay Heather." He turned from the door just as I was opening my mouth to yell "Feather!" at him. "Joyce! Mia's friend is here to see you." He turned his back and closed the door in my face.

"Did that really just happen?" I asked Jake, looking at him in disbelief. Before he could answer, the door opened again.

"Oh shit," Mia's mother swore, then closed the door and fumbled with the chain. "How does this stupid thing work, Len?"

"You have to slide it to the right, ma'am," Jake called through the door, helpfully. I smacked him on the arm. Joyce managed to unlatch the chain and open the door.

"Sorry about that. Hi, Feather. Hi, Jake."

"Hi, Joyce. We're looking for Mia. She isn't answering her phone. Do you have any idea where she is?"

"Mia? No. She left last night."

"I know that, Joyce. What I don't know is where she is now. Have you heard from her?" I asked.

"No. She's probably off sulking somewhere."

"Sulking?" I looked at her, trying to stay calm.

"You know Mia. Always in a mood about something," Joyce waved her hand in the air. "She makes a fuss and leaves for a day or two. She'll be back. She always comes back eventually when she realizes no one is going to chase her."

I chose my words very carefully. "And what would she be in a mood about this time, Joyce?" I asked.

"Oh, she made up some crazy story about Leonard. That he was touching her or something. She was obviously lying to get attention. I told her if she wanted to live under my roof, she had to respect my husband."

"So you kicked her out in the middle of the night with nowhere to go?" I asked, my eyes narrowing.

"She could have gone to your house," she said.

"But she didn't!" I told her, my voice going up an octave. "You threw her out with Indigenous girls going missing or being killed all over the city!"

"Mia can take of herself, Feather!" she snapped at me. "And she shouldn't have lied to me."

"She didn't lie to you, Joyce." I was beyond being nice now. "Are you really that blind?"

"What are you talking about?"

"Leonard has been touching her for months! She had to get a lock for her bedroom door to keep him out." I could feel my face getting red as Jake reached for my arm.

"Let's go, Feather. They don't know where she is. I don't think they even care," he said.

"You're right! I don't care! That girl is a liar. Making up nasty stories about poor Leonard. That man has done nothing but care for her as if she was his own daughter." Joyce crossed her arms over her substantial chest.

"Oh really? Her stepfather cares for her so much that he rubs his crotch against her. He cares so much that he grabs her ass and brushes against her chest," I yelled. I had completely lost it now. She didn't give a damn about Mia.

"You believe her lies?" she asked.

"I saw it, Joyce! More than once. I saw what he was doing to her. I told her to go to you and look what good that did her. How dare you treat her like that?" I shouted as Jake began to pull me towards the car. "He kicked her door in to get to her!"

"Get off my property!" Joyce yelled. "You're a liar! You're as bad as she is!"

"And you're a useless excuse for a mother," Jake called over his shoulder, his voice calm and steady. "You're trash, Joyce. You ignore what's right in front of your face. You knew what he was doing to Mia, didn't you? That's right," he nodded at her. "Feather told me. Did you just let it go because that was the only way you could hang onto him?" he asked. I stared at him and then at Joyce, who looked shocked. "You should be the one who goes missing. You'd be doing everyone a favour."

I stared at him wordlessly. His face was completely blank but there was something menacing about his tone. It sounded as if he wanted to make her disappear.

I was shaking as he led me to the car and opened the door for me. "Get in, Feather. Let's get out of here." My hands shook as I took my phone out of my bag and looked at it. Nothing. I leaned forward, trying to catch my breath. Jake got in the driver's seat.

"Can we go to the police department?" I asked. He nodded and started the car.

"I'm sorry about that, Feather. But she deserved it."

"Yeah, just . . . drive," I said, resting my forehead against the window and closing my eyes.

CHAPTER 20
RUNAWAY

The ride to the police station was far from quiet. I was sure Jake was upset too but I assumed he was keeping it together for my sake. He drummed his fingers on the steering wheel and listened to me ranting.

"Can you believe that woman?" I asked him. I didn't wait for an answer. "How dare she talk about Mia like that? She made me furious!"

"Me too," Jake said simply.

"Not only does she not believe her own daughter when she says her scumbag husband is molesting her, but she kicks Mia out in the middle of the night? Then she doesn't hear from her, but hey! No big deal. Because her daughter's just a liar! And she'll come back eventually. I wanted to smack that self-righteous look right off her face."

"I know, babe. I was ready to punch her stepdad too."

"God, they're awful. I mean, I knew Leonard was skeevy but I always thought her mom was okay. I never should have left her there alone or told her to talk to her mother." I looked out the window. "And now she's gone." I wiped a tear off my face.

"We'll find her, Feather." Jake took my hand in his and kissed it, the way he knows makes my heart flutter.

"How do you know?" I asked him. Pleaded with him, really.

"Because I have faith that everything will work out," he said, smiling softly.

"I wish I did."

We parked in the visitors' section of the police department parking lot and walked into the reception area. It was mostly quiet except for one guy who was obviously drunk, slouched on a bench. He belched loudly and scratched at his crotch. I wrinkled my nose and walked up to the officer manning the reception desk. He looked up from his computer Solitaire game.

"Can I help you?" he asked.

"We need to report a missing person," I told him.

He looked at me closely, and then picked up the phone. "Perkins, I've got someone who wants to report a missing person. Okay. Thanks." He looked at us again and gestured to the bench. "Have a seat. Someone will be with you in a minute."

I glanced over at the occupant of the bench, who farted explosively. "I think we'll stand. Thanks." I snuck a look at Jake, who was pointedly looking away from the drunken guy, his face neutral. We stared around the room, reading the "Most Wanted" posters and "Missing" posters on the wall. So many Aboriginal faces looked back at me from that wall. I sighed and turned as the sound of heavy footsteps came towards us.

"Hi . . ." My voice trailed off as I took in the officer standing in front of me, a large coffee in his hand. Oh. Shit.

"Well hello again." He took a large gulp of his coffee. "Can I get you anything?" he asked. "Coffee? Maybe a donut?"

"Listen, I'm sorry for losing my temper with you and your partner." Jake nudged me. "And for the donut comment. I was upset about my friend. I didn't mean it. You were being decent and you didn't deserve that."

The cop nodded and sipped at his coffee again. "Ah. Hot!" He gestured for us to follow him back to his office. He sat down behind a large wooden desk and nodded towards the chairs on the other side. We settled into the seats and I leaned forward, resting my elbows on my knees, studying the name-plate on his desk. Constable Perkins.

"So what can I do for you?" he asked. I looked at Jake, and then took a deep breath.

"My . . . our . . . our friend is missing."

"Okay." He started typing on his computer. "Name?"

"Mia Joseph." He glanced up at me, then back to his computer screen.

"Age?"

"Seventeen."

"When was the last time she was seen?" he asked.

"I'm not sure. But I talked to her around midnight. She had a fight with her mom and someone was picking her up."

He stopped typing. "Have you tried calling her parents?" he asked.

"Yeah." I glanced over at Jake. "We went there first. They don't know where she is. They're the ones who kicked her out!"

"Her parents kicked her out?" he asked. "Why?"

"Why does this matter?" I asked, getting frustrated. "Just find her!"

"Have they kicked her out before?" he asked.

"No! I don't think so," I told him.

"But she's run away before," he stated, leaning back in his chair.

"She doesn't run away! She goes to the rec centre sometimes. Just to get away from her stepfather." It was taking all of my self-control not to dive over the desk and throttle him.

Why wouldn't he help me? I looked at Jake pleadingly.

"Her stepfather gets . . . handsy. So she takes off for a day or two to get a break. It wasn't like that this time. She got into a fight with her mom and she kicked her out," Jake told him.

"Right!" I broke in. "She called and said someone was picking her up and she was going to lie low for a day or two to figure things out."

"Who picked her up?" Perkins asked.

I shrugged. "She didn't tell me." I stopped and looked at the floor. "I should have asked her." I looked up and caught Perkins looking at me sympathetically. I was surprised. Especially since I had yelled at him at the school.

"Listen, you can file a missing person report but she'll be considered a habitual runaway."

"But she always answers her phone or lets me know she's okay. And I can't reach her!" I looked at him pleadingly. "If she's okay, then why can't I reach her?"

"I don't know," he admitted. "Look, I can file the paperwork. That's not a problem. Let's start there." He tapped away at his keyboard again.

We gave him all the information we could come up with but we had no idea who had seen her last or where she had gone. I took Perkins's card and we left. As we stepped back out into the sunshine, I squinted and shaded my face with my hand, reaching into my bag for my sunglasses. Jake held the car door open for me and I settled myself back into the passenger seat. The sun was beating through the windshield. As soon as Jake got in and started the car, I put the window down and leaned out, like a dog on the highway.

"Where to now?" Jake asked, pulling out of the parking lot and accelerating so my hair began blowing and whipping around my face. I pulled my head into the car and tried to smooth it back down away from my face. I pulled a strand out of my mouth before answering.

"Let's try the rec centre," I said. Jake nodded and signalled, then made a left-hand turn towards the river.

CHAPTER 21
SAFE HAVEN

The rec centre was more than just a place for homeless kids to stay or teens to crash when they got into fights with their parents. It was a sanctuary. Kids could come and spend an hour or a few days — whatever they needed. It didn't matter where they came from or what they did on the street. They could get a hot meal, a shower and a bed if they needed it or come in and play basketball or pool or watch TV. No judgment. No questions asked. It was a much-needed haven in our community.

I hadn't spent much time there myself, but Mia had taken me a few times to hang out and play board games when she didn't feel like going home. It was clean and there were lockers where you could keep your stuff safe. Overstuffed sofas and chairs were in the main room along with tables where you could play cards or do your homework.

Michael was a tall, unimposing guy who had a smile on his face every time I saw him. He had run the rec centre for years and treated every kid as if he or she was the most important person in the world. That's why they came back and that's why they talked to him when they felt as if they couldn't talk to anyone else. Mia adored him, and when she brought me to the rec centre with her, he had made me feel incredibly welcome.

When we pulled into the parking lot, I saw Michael shooting hoops with a few boys who were significantly shorter than he was. He did an easy layup, his long braid flying behind him, and passed the ball to one of the kids. He looked up as Jake and I approached, and I waved.

"Tanisi, Feather. Good to see you," he called, catching a pass and dribbling it before passing to another kid.

"Hi, Michael," I replied. "Namoya miwasin. It's not good," I repeated. "Could I talk to you for a minute?" Michael was Cree, like me.

"Yeah, of course. Boys, I'll be back in a few." He waved to a small boy wearing a Toronto Raptors jersey who was watching from the sidelines. "Thomas, can you do me a favour and sub in for me? Take it easy on them though, okay?" He ruffled the boy's hair. Thomas grinned at him and ran onto the court. Michael grabbed a bottle of water and sat down at a nearby picnic table. He smiled at me and nodded at Jake, holding out his hand. "Hi, there. I'm Michael." Jake reached out and shook it.

"Jake. How're you doing?"

"Good, thanks. So what can I do for you?" he asked, chugging his water and then wiping the sweat off his face with his sleeve.

"Did Mia come here last night?" I asked, my fingers crossed for his answer.

"Last night? I'm not sure. Definitely not before eight o'clock. I left then and she wasn't here."

"No, it would have been later. Sometime after midnight."

"Ah. Well, I wasn't here but we lock the door at ten." He looked between Jake and me.

"So she wouldn't have been able to get in after that?" Jake asked.

"No. Well, she could have," he said.

"How?" I asked, leaning forward.

"We have a policy in place now. With all the missing and murdered Indigenous girls . . . we have an emergency number on the door. If anyone, girl or boy, feels threatened, they can call and whoever is on duty at night will answer. If we have a spot for them, it's theirs."

"And if you don't have a spot?" Jake asked him.

Michael shrugged.

"It hasn't been an issue yet. There was one night we were full and a girl called after hours. She said she thought someone was following her under the bridge. She said she could hear his footsteps and hear him breathing, but when she called out, he wouldn't answer. It scared her so she came to the centre." He took another drink from his water bottle. "We didn't have a bed but she was really freaked out. I gave her a blanket and pillow and let her sleep on one of the couches."

"That was nice of you," Jake told him. "So how can we find out if Mia came last night? Do you have a sign-in sheet?"

Michael shook his head.

"No. We used to but the kids didn't like it. They left fake names so we got rid of it. But I could ask Larry. He was here overnight."

"Could you call him now?" I asked.

Michael looked at us, puzzled.

"Mind if I ask why?"

"We haven't been able to reach her since she left her house last night. She's not answering her phone. She was supposed to call me this morning but I haven't heard from her." I sighed deeply. "No one has."

A shadow of concern darkened Michael's features. "What

about her parents? Have you spoken to them?"

I nodded.

"They're the reason she left. I convinced her to talk to her mother . . ." My voice cracked. Jake put an arm around me as Michael raised his eyebrows questioningly.

"She was having problems at home," Jake said. "And it was escalating." He looked over at me. "Feather told her that she should talk to her mom, but they got into a fight." Although vague, his description was accurate.

"And now we don't know where she is. Could you please call and find out if she made it here last night?" I begged.

Michael nodded and quickly fished his cell phone out of his pocket. He scrolled through his contacts and then held it up to his ear. And waited. "*Voicemail,*" he mouthed.

"Yeah, hey Larry. It's Michael. Listen, can you call me back as soon as you get this? I'm trying to find out if Mia Joseph was at the centre last night. It's really important that you get back to me as soon as you can, okay? Thanks a lot." He hung up and looked over at us. "He's probably asleep. If you want to give me your number, I'll let you know as soon as I hear from him." I gave Michael my number and watched to make sure he put it in his phone correctly. "Please call me as soon as you hear from him," I pleaded.

"I will. Let me know if you hear from her in the meantime, okay?" We promised that we would and headed back to the car.

"Where do you want to go now?" Jake asked gently.

"I don't know," I told him. I was at a loss. I had no idea where to look for her. "Can you drop me off at home? I need my laptop." He nodded and signalled, turning towards home.

CHAPTER 22

THE ONLY MOVING THING WAS THE EYE OF THE BLACKBIRD

This one, this little blackbird, had fallen into his lap unexpectedly. He wasn't ready. He didn't cover his tracks like he usually did. But he couldn't resist her. She was a fighter.

He liked that.

He smiled.

He may not have been able to cover his tracks but he had an ace up his sleeve. He almost couldn't believe his luck.

He picked up his phone and dialed a number, drumming his fingers on the table and humming as it rang.

"Hello?" He straightened up in his chair, smiling. "I just saw a boy dragging a girl into his car. Yeah, he hit her too. I think he had a knife. He got away before I could do anything. Yes, I can describe the car. I wrote down the license plate number too."

CHAPTER 23
COLD CASES

"I keep forgetting your brother is home." Jake nodded towards Kiowa's car as he pulled into my driveway.

"Yeah. I guess he'll be heading back to school in the next day or two."

"What has he been doing since he's been back? Studying?" he asked.

"I have no idea. I haven't seen that much of him. Other than having dinner together most nights, he hasn't really been around much. Hanging out with some of his old friends, I guess." I shrugged. The whereabouts of my brother and his social circle were hardly at the top of my list of things to worry about right now.

"Are you coming in?" I asked him, opening the car door.

"I think I'll go talk to Ben. He knows where Carli went when her foster mom's place got too loud. Maybe he can help us come up with some places to look for Mia."

"That's a really good idea," I told him. If anyone could help us figure out where Mia may be hiding out, it was Ben. "Maybe you could take Matt with you?" I suggested, trying to subtly play peacemaker. I watched that look of distaste cross his face again before he smiled.

"Yeah. Maybe." I already knew he wasn't going to call Matt. I tried to shrug off my unease.

"Call me after you talk to Ben." I turned my head so his kiss landed on my cheek. I saw the hurt on his face as he backed out of the driveway.

I opened the front door and walked into an eerily silent house. Despite the silence, it didn't feel empty for some reason.

"Kiowa?" I called out. No response. I walked through the kitchen where there was a fresh pot of coffee steaming on the counter. Weird. I kept walking, calling to Kiowa. I stood in the centre of the deserted living room and threw my hands up. Maybe someone had picked him up. I shrugged and walked back towards the kitchen. I passed the door to the garage and stopped. I heard the low murmur of my brother's voice. I walked closer to the door, unable to make out what he was saying or who he was talking to. Then I shook my head. It wasn't any of my business. I started to walk away when I heard him yell. The hair on the back of my neck stood up. Kiowa never yells.

"Well figure it out! I need to know what happened!" The door flew open, hitting the wall hard. I jumped backwards. Kiowa stormed into the house, holding his phone against his ear. He stopped dead when he saw me. "Just call me when you know something," he muttered into the phone. He hung up and looked at me. "So," he said. He looked awful. He was pale and unshaven, his eyes red-rimmed.

"Are you okay?" I asked.

"Yeah. Well no," he said, running a hand over his sand-paper chin. "Maybe something I ate," he mumbled.

"Coffee probably isn't the best idea then," I said mildly.

"Yeah, I know."

"Who were you yelling at? Sounded serious." I glanced down at his phone. He didn't meet my eyes as he pulled his phone away from my gaze.

"It was nothing."

"It didn't sound like nothing, Ki." I bent over, trying to get him to look at me. "Are you in some kind of trouble?"

"No! Of course not." He finally met my eyes and I could see he was telling the truth. I relaxed slightly.

"Then what is it?" I asked. He looked like he was debating what to tell me.

"It's . . . something at school I have to deal with." He looked away. That usually meant he was hiding something. I sighed. Everyone seemed to be hiding something lately.

"Is there anything I can do to help?" I asked him. He shook his head, and then gave me a quick, one-armed hug.

"Thanks, but no. Unfortunately I don't think there is." He scratched at his face again and walked past me into the kitchen. I turned and watched him take a mug out of the cupboard and pour himself a cup of black coffee. He carried it out into the backyard with him and fell heavily into a chair, sipping at it and staring at the fence.

His phone rang, forgotten on the counter where he had left it. Without thinking, I picked it up just as Kiowa burst into the room and nearly dislocated my arm tearing it away from me.

"Hey!" I glared at him.

"Don't touch my stuff!" He stormed out of the kitchen but paused at the doorway to his room and turned back to look at me. "Sorry," he muttered before answering his call. "Yeah."

I rubbed my arm and tiptoed towards the door, wishing I had seen who was calling before being manhandled by my brother. He had his back to me, mumbling quietly into his phone. I idly picked up a magazine and leafed through it, watching him.

"Yeah, okay. Thanks." He stood for a second and looked around his room, clearly unaware that I was watching him. He walked over to his closet and shoved his phone under the sweaters that were sitting on the top shelf. What on earth? He closed his closet and I quickly stepped away so he couldn't tell I was spying on him. If I'd had any doubt that my brother was hiding something, it was gone.

But I had Mia to worry about right now. And something was going on with my brother too. Once I found Mia, I wouldn't be so quick to let him and his hidden phone off the hook.

× × ×

I grabbed something to eat and headed into my bedroom, closing the door firmly behind me. I sat down on my bed, opened my laptop and looked at the screen. The background was a picture of Jake and me hugging, with Mia photo-bombing us in the background. I smiled at the face she was making, her fingers pulling at the sides of her mouth with her tongue sticking out. I opened the Internet browser and stopped, my fingers hovering over the keyboard. I wasn't exactly sure what I was looking for or where to start.

I took a deep breath and typed in "missing and murdered Indigenous women" and hit enter. Holy shit! 225,000 results? I guess I'd start with Amnesty International since I actually knew who they were. I sat and read for the next hour, my snack sitting forgotten beside me.

Over a thousand women and girls, all murdered right here in Canada in just over thirty years. Even though I had heard my mother tell me the numbers, it still shocked me. And 105 were still missing. I think what really stopped me in my tracks was the realization that Carli was now on that list too. The articles on the CBC website were just as terrifying. There were 230 unsolved cases and so much violence. And I guess Carli was 231. Violence in the lives of these women and girls before they were killed or went missing. More violence that destroyed their lives or ended them entirely. Some of the women were prostitutes and drug users. Some were simply girls who disappeared without a trace. Walking to school. Leaving the mall. And some of them were just hanging out at the wrong place at the wrong time.

All those families left behind without answers. I wondered if we'd ever have any answers about Carli. Would Ben ever have any closure? The police didn't seem very interested in finding out the truth.

And where was Mia? Please God, I breathed, don't let her be number 106. I scrolled down and saw face after face staring back at me from the screen.

Missing.

Missing.

Murdered.

Missing.

Murdered.

Murdered.

I glanced down at my phone. Mia, where the hell are you?

× × ×

I dialed Jake as soon as I closed my laptop. The second I heard him pick up, I launched into a monologue about what I had found out.

"You won't believe this!" I told him. "I started searching online and Mia and Carli . . . they're just the tip of the iceberg, Jake. I knew there were a bunch of Indigenous women missing or killed, but I didn't know it was this big! The RCMP released a report on the missing and murdered Indigenous women, right? Yeah, I know. But listen. So the report came back and there have been over a thousand deaths, Jake! Yes, that many!" I was pacing around my bedroom now. "And 105 women still missing. Well . . . Carli was 106 until they found her. And . . . I guess Mia is 106 now. If she's actually missing. No. I haven't heard anything from Michael. But Jake . . . why aren't newspapers reporting more of these disappearances? How can there be so many unsolved murders in one group? Why doesn't anyone care? Why isn't someone doing something? Why are they letting more girls go missing?"

I heard the doorbell ring midway through my rant but I ignored it. A minute later, I heard it again.

"Is that the doorbell?" Jake asked.

"Yeah. It's okay. Kiowa is home. He can get it." I took the phone away from my mouth and yelled to him. "Ki! Get the door, please! I'm on the phone! Sorry about that," I told Jake. I lay down on my bed and sighed deeply. "I just can't get my head around it, Jake. How do the police, no, the government! How does the government let something like this happen and do absolutely nothing to stop it?"

I heard a thump from downstairs. Then a muffled shout. There was definitely a scuffle going on down there. I dropped the phone to my side and started out my bedroom door, Jake's tinny voice sounding a million miles away as he continued talking — something about the ineptitude of the police and racism — and I broke into a run when I heard Kiowa scream my name.

CHAPTER 24
PRIME SUSPECT

"Feather!"

I almost flew down the stairs, my phone hanging by my side with Jake's faint voice calling, "Feather? Feather? Are you still there? What's going on?"

I ran through the living room, banging my thigh on the sofa so hard that I nearly went down, but I kept running towards the front hall where I saw my brother, pressed face-first into the wall.

"Kiowa!" I screamed, throwing myself at the police officer who was cuffing him. "Stop it! What the hell are you doing to my brother?" I dropped my phone and went at him with two hands.

"Feather, stop!" Kiowa yelled. The cop smirked at his partner and then reached out and shoved me. First my shoulder hit the wall, then my head. I crumpled to the floor, holding the side of my face.

"I'll arrest you for assaulting an officer if you try that again," the cop said. His partner stepped forward.

"Okay. That's enough." He held out a hand to me. I looked up at him warily, vaguely registering Kiowa asking if I was okay under his breath. I nodded at him and took the cop's hand. He helped me up.

"You should have left the stupid bitch on her knees where she belongs." The cop holding Kiowa laughed. He pulled Kiowa away from the wall and shoved him forward.

"Why are you arresting him?" I asked, directing the question at the officer who had helped me up. "What did he do?" Before he could answer, Officer Dickhead piped in.

"We're arresting him for the suspected abduction of Mia Joseph"

"What? What are you talking about? Why would you arrest him for that? That's insane! Kiowa, what are they talking about?"

Kiowa opened his mouth and then closed it again.

"Your brother was seen with her last night around the time she disappeared."

"No, he was home last night. Kiowa, tell them!" I remembered hearing the door open and close while I was on the phone with Mia. Was that Kiowa coming home or going out? "Ki?" I asked.

"Feather, just stop talking!" he hissed, not meeting my eyes. My mouth dropped open. The cops started to pull him out the door, and not very gently.

"What should I do, Ki?" I asked, my eyes filling with tears. I wiped at them angrily, my head throbbing where I had hit the wall.

"I didn't hurt her, Feather! You know that! Call Mom!" he yelled over his shoulder as he was muscled out the door and onto the front lawn. "Feather, call Mom!" he shouted again.

"I will! I'll call her right now!" I yelled back, looking down at my empty hands for my phone. The neighbours were out on their lawns, staring at Kiowa being dragged to the squad car and whispering to one another. I saw at least three people with cell phones filming him. Where the hell was my phone? I stayed in the doorway watching as they put Kiowa in the car. Our eyes met through the car window. He looked broken.

What made them think he had something to do with Mia's disappearance?

I closed the door behind me before the neighbours could start asking questions. I saw my phone lying on the floor where I had dropped it moments before.

"Feather, what the hell is going on?" Jake's voice sounded far away as I picked up the phone.

"Jake . . . they just arrested Kiowa. I have to go. I have to call my mom."

"They . . . wait. For what?" he asked before I could hang up.

"They said he was with Mia last night." My voice broke and I took a breath, willing myself to stay calm.

"That's insane! Call your mom. I'm on my way over."

"Okay. Thanks. And Jake?"

"Yeah?"

"Please hurry." I hung up and took another deep breath. I had no idea what I was going to tell my mother. I hit the number three on my phone and waited, listening to it ring on the other end. I almost hoped that I'd get her voicemail. Then I remembered Kiowa's face in the car.

"Mom? It's me. Something happened to Kiowa."

× × ×

How do you tell your mother about the arrest of her child for the possible abduction of your best friend?

I tried to explain what was going on to my increasingly frantic mother but I wasn't even sure myself. I had no idea why they suspected Kiowa. I said as much before my mom hung up, saying she would rush to the police station. I was left pacing and waiting for Jake.

I was popping some Advil and getting ice for the rapidly forming lump on my head when I heard the front door fly open.

"Feather!" he called out.

"In here." I was wrapping ice in a hand towel when he rushed into the kitchen.

"Hey! What happened?" he asked. "Are you okay?"

"Yeah. I'll live," I told him. "One of the cops didn't appreciate me jumping on him."

"So he hit you?"

"No. He pushed me away and I fell into the wall." I saw his face darken with anger.

Jake took the ice from me and led me over to a kitchen chair. He pressed the ice gently against my head. I winced.

"Sorry." He pushed a lock of hair off my face. "So why do they think Kiowa did something to Mia?"

I sighed.

"I don't know. I don't get why he'd be a suspect. But they said he was seen with her before she disappeared."

"But why would your brother be with her?" he asked.

I shrugged.

"I have no idea. I told them he was home but . . ." I glanced at Jake. "I'm not so sure."

"Why?" he asked.

"I heard the door. I don't know if he was coming or going. I just don't know. Anyway, they didn't seem to care what I had to say."

"So . . . he could have been with her," Jake said.

"No. Why would he be?" I asked.

"I don't know. But you can't be his alibi if you didn't see him at home and don't know for sure he wasn't with her."

I paused. I couldn't really be sure. But either way, I felt confident he didn't have anything to do with Mia.

We sat mostly in silence, waiting for my mom to get home from the police station. I had fallen asleep in front of the TV with my head on Jake's shoulder when she finally came in.

"Feather?" Jake shook me gently. I opened my eyes just as my mom walked into the room. She saw us on the couch and burst into tears. We both jumped up. I hugged her tightly while Jake slipped past us to make tea.

It took my mom a while to stop crying. "Is Ki okay?" I asked her as we sat down on the couch together. Jake walked in with a tray holding a pot of steaming tea, milk, sugar and three cups. He handed one to my mom.

"Thanks, Jake. He's all right, I guess," she answered me. "I only got to see him for a minute."

"Did you speak to the police?" Jake asked her, pouring tea into her cup.

"Yes." She blew on her tea.

"So what did they say? Why are they blaming him? When is he coming home?" I asked in one breath.

"I don't know, Feather," she said. "He goes before a judge tomorrow and hopefully they'll set bail so we can bring him home then."

× × ×

The next day was brighter and more cheerful than I felt it had any right to be. I scowled out the window, and then yawned widely. I had barely slept, and from the looks of my mother, she hadn't either.

Jake arrived wearing khakis, a blue button-down shirt that made his eyes pop brightly and a tie. He was balancing a box of donuts and a tray of take-out coffee cups.

"I thought you could use this," he said, handing a coffee to each of us and opening the box of donuts.

"Thanks, Jake," I said and gratefully tore into a maple dip.

× × ×

I could still taste the sweetness of the maple glaze on my lips as we sat down outside the courtroom. It took over an hour for our turn, and we shuffled in together with the lawyer that my mother had hired for Kiowa. He smiled and waved at us as he entered, looking better than I expected.

"Your Honour," the other lawyer began smoothly before Kiowa had even sat down. "I would like to respectfully request that bail be withheld for Kiowa Bedard. I believe strongly that he is a danger to himself and to the community at large. We have reason to believe he abducted Mia Joseph and quite possibly others. With the epidemic of missing and murdered Indigenous women in this city, I believe it is our responsibility to investigate the disappearance of this girl fully before we allow him the opportunity to run. We believe that Miss Joseph is, in fact, dead and Mr. Bedard is the prime suspect."

I heard a gasp of shock from my mother and turned to look at Jake. His face registered the same horror I was sure was written all over my own.

"Your Honour!" Kiowa's lawyer interjected. "There is no

evidence to back up this claim. My client is innocent. He presents no danger to anyone and should be released immediately into his mother's custody."

My mother gripped my hand so tightly, it was turning purple.

"Your Honour, not only is this man a danger to the community, he's a flight risk," the other lawyer interrupted. I loathed her. My brother wasn't a danger and he wouldn't run away! I wanted to scream. The lawyer continued, "He has family on a reserve in northern Ontario and I believe he may leave the province if given the opportunity. The RCMP has reported that the vast majority of crimes perpetrated against Aboriginal women are by members of their own communities too," she continued.

"Mr. Bedard's family is here today, Your Honour." I looked at the judge and willed him to let Kiowa go. His lawyer continued. "He has a close family and a supportive community right here in Winnipeg. There is absolutely no risk in releasing my client to his mother."

"Enough!" the judge said tiredly. "I've heard enough from both of you. Mr. Bedard, you are to enter the Winnipeg Remand Centre until your trial." He slammed the gavel down and looked at the bailiff. "Next case, please."

As the guards took a shocked Kiowa away, my mother cried and I held Jake tightly. What had just happened? Kiowa met my eyes briefly. Then he was gone.

CHAPTER 25
FREE BIRD

He stared intently at the newspaper, and then laughed violently.

"Local Man Arrested in Disappearance of Teen" the headline read.

He was in the clear. He looked towards the basement door where he could hear a voice calling out thinly.

"Help."

CHAPTER 26
SUSPECT LIST

A prison bus took Kiowa to the Winnipeg Remand Centre, to wait out the time before his trial. I still couldn't believe there was going to be a trial. Getting a trial date could take months. The only good thing about Kiowa being at the WRC was that we could go and visit him. We immediately made an appointment to see him the following day.

As soon as I saw the imposing building through the car window, I knew I wasn't ready to see my brother there. Truthfully, it looked like an office building. But knowing the inside would look different, I couldn't do it. I couldn't look at Kiowa in a neon orange jumpsuit through a dingy pane of scratched-up Plexiglas. Okay, so it was entirely possible that we'd all be sitting around a table playing cards and chatting, but I wasn't ready to take a chance that I'd be talking through a handset that smelled like the hundreds of people who had used it before me. What if they brought him out in shackles?

I was also afraid to hear the reason why the police thought he had something to do with Mia's disappearance. I wasn't stupid enough to believe it was all some big misunderstanding. Obviously, they had some reason to think he was guilty. I didn't think he was involved. I really didn't, I told myself. But I just wasn't ready to see my brother locked up. I said as much to my mom.

"It's not going to be like some prison show on television, Feather." She tried to reassure me but I had an overactive imagination and I had reason to worry.

So, I waited in the car, trying to ignore the disappointed but understanding look I got from my mother. It didn't make me feel any better about missing the visit to know that she understood why.

I spent some time googling information on the WRC. I should have done that before I declined the visit. My horrible vision of walking in and finding a brother I didn't recognize, covered in prison ink and refusing to talk to me without calling me a bitch and swearing excessively seemed over the top now. Especially given the short time he had been in remand.

I put my phone in my bag and pulled out a pen and a crumpled receipt for a book I had bought a couple of weeks ago. It had been a gift for Mia. My heart twisted. I turned the receipt over and wrote "SUSPECTS" on the back. I chewed the cap of my pen and thought hard before I started writing.

1. Leonard!!

Mia's skeevy stepfather had to be at the top of the list. He had a motive and he had the opportunity. I added a couple of exclamation marks after his name.

2. Michael

This one was tougher. I liked the guy who ran the rec centre. But Mia and Carli had both spent time there. And, truthfully, I knew nothing about him.

I paused for a second, then wrote:

3. Larry

I had never even met the guy who worked the night Mia

went missing, but if Michael had the opportunity, so did he.

I chewed my pen again before continuing to the names I didn't want to add to the list.

4. Kiowa

It killed me to write my brother's name on the list but a part of me knew that the police believed he was with Mia that night for a reason. I just didn't know what it was yet.

5. Jake

For some reason, my boyfriend's name was easier to add to the list than my brother's was. I had seen a side of him recently that I didn't like and, hard as it was to admit, it proved that I didn't know him nearly as well as I thought I did. I remembered how he had pulled my hair and forced my head back . . . I didn't want to, but I imagined him doing that to Mia or Carli. Thinking of Carli made me add the next name to my list.

6. Ben

I couldn't really see gentle Ben hurting anyone. But he knew both Mia and Carli well and he knew where they liked to hang out.

I folded the list in half, then unfolded it and added another name.

7. Joyce

Mia's mom. I couldn't imagine Joyce killing Carli but who knows how far she might go to get rid of anyone who threatened her relationship with Leonard.

8. ???

If the RCMP report was reliable, then I'd have to consider it was someone Mia knew. But the fact was, it could have been a stranger. Both Mia and Carli had knives. They knew there were some dangerous people down by the river at night. What if it was one of the guys they saw down there?

× × ×

The driver's side door opened, scaring the hell out of me. I jumped and shrieked. I admit that for a second, I thought a convict had escaped and was going to steal our car to get away with me still in it. Obviously, it was just my mom coming back from her visit.

"Are you okay?" my mother asked. I nodded at her and stuffed my pen and the list back in my bag.

"How did it go?" I asked. "Is Kiowa okay?"

"He's okay. Hanging in there. " She rummaged in her purse for a tissue and blew her nose loudly. She turned towards me and tried to smile.

"Mom, are you all right?" I asked her softly. I hated seeing her cry. It made me well up too.

"Yeah, it was just so hard. Seeing him in that place . . ." She took a deep breath. "I'm okay now. I understand why you wanted to stay in the car, though. Ki understood too," she told me.

"He did? Really?" I asked her, reaching for her hand.

"Yes, he did. He'll be happy to see you whenever you're ready," she said, turning in her seat to smile gently at me.

"Is he really all right? Did he say anything about why they arrested him?" I asked.

"He did," she admitted. "But he said he really wanted to tell you in person."

"Oh . . . okay," I said, settling back into my seat and fastening my seatbelt. "Can we go home now? I hate the look of this place." I shuddered.

"Definitely," my mom said, starting the car.

CHAPTER 27
THE TRUTH HURTS

I had been neglecting my homework. For good reason, obviously. But the fact was, I had a huge English assignment due and a math test to study for. I'd have to pull a few all-nighters to catch up.

I sat hunched over my desk, trying to decipher my math textbook when my phone rang. I figured it was Jake, so I didn't check the number before answering the call.

"Hello?"

A recorded voice said, "You have a call from an inmate at the Winnipeg Remand Centre. If you would like to accept this call, please press 1 now. If you wish to decline, please hang up." I pressed 1.

"Kiowa?"

"Feather! I wasn't sure if you'd accept my call. Hi!" My brother's voice never sounded better to me than it did at that moment.

"Of course I'd take your call! I'm so sorry about this afternoon, Ki. I kind of freaked out when we got to the . . . the uh . . ." I trailed off.

"Jail? Prison? Facility?" Kiowa replied. "It's okay, Feather. I know where I am."

"How are you, Ki? Are you okay? No one's hurt you, have they?" I asked.

"Nah. There are a lot of Native guys in here. I just hang with them. No one bothers us. The guards leave you alone as long as you follow the rules and don't cause any trouble," he told me.

"Good. That's really good. I'm so glad you called me. I'll definitely come in next time, I swear."

"It's okay," he said.

"Kiowa?"

"Yeah?"

"Why are you in there? I mean . . . why do the cops think you had something to do with Mia's disappearance?" I asked him.

Kiowa let out a long, low breath. "Feather, there's something we should have told you."

"I don't get why they think you were with her that night." Wait . . . did he say "we"? "What do you mean 'we,' Kiowa? Who's 'we'?" I asked him.

"Mia and I," he answered. "Listen, Feather . . ."

"Mia and . . . wait. What are you saying, Kiowa?"

"We were seeing each other, Feather," he said finally.

"No you weren't," I said. "She'd have told me if she was seeing someone."

"We wanted to. I mean, at first we figured there was no point in saying anything. Not if we were just hanging out."

"So what happened?" I asked.

"It turned into something else. Something more. By then, we couldn't figure out how to tell you."

"You're my brother! And she's my best friend!" I was angry. With him. And with Mia. "How could you go behind my back like that?" I asked him.

"I didn't mean for anything to happen, Feather. I swear. Neither did Mia."

"But how did it happen?"

"She came over one night looking for you last summer. Her stepfather had been trying to push his way into her room again." He sounded angry as he said this. Despite my feelings of anger and betrayal, I could hear that he genuinely cared about her. "You were out with Jake, so I invited her in and we sat up and talked for hours. And that was it, Feather. We just talked. After that, she called me or texted me sometimes and then we started talking late at night. I didn't mean to, but I found myself looking forward to talking to her. We made plans to hang out sometimes at the rec centre or back at the campus. Just as friends." He paused for a moment and I had the sudden realization that on some of the nights she was down by the river, she was actually with my brother.

"So when did she stop being just your friend, Kiowa?" I wasn't angry now. I could hear in his voice that he was agonizing over this. I knew my brother and Mia well enough to know this had nothing to do with me. They'd never hurt me on purpose.

"I don't know, exactly. One minute we were friends hanging out, and the next thing I knew, I couldn't stop thinking about her. I'm so sorry, Feather. We never meant to hurt you."

"I know." And I did. "So the police obviously know you were seeing her. Are they just blaming the boyfriend?"

"Not exactly," he said.

"So?" It suddenly occurred to me what he must be talking about. "You're the one who picked her up that night, aren't you?"

He sighed again. "Yeah. She called me, crying. You know

what happened. I told her I'd come and get her and bring her back to our place," he said.

"When I was on the phone with her, I heard you leaving. But you didn't bring her back."

"No. I didn't even come home. I was mad at her. We got into an argument." His voice broke.

"About what?" I asked.

"She wanted to go to the rec centre for the night. I didn't want her down there. I thought she should stay with us but she wouldn't. She said she wanted some time to think things over; she had a lot to work out for herself. She hated that we were lying to you, Feather. But she also felt like we were both pushing her. Me to keep things secret and . . . I guess you and she had it out about her stepfather?"

"We did," I said softly, feeling an overwhelming stab of guilt. " So did you take her to the centre?"

"Yeah, I dropped her off at the rec centre. She didn't want me to come in. She was upset about her mom and she wanted to be alone. I dropped her off. I didn't even wait to see if she went inside." His voice lowered. "I was still mad so I drove around for awhile. I turned my ringer off because I wasn't ready to talk to Mia. I ended up close to campus so I went to my dorm and went to bed."

"So she did make it to the rec centre?" I asked.

"Yeah, she did. But something must have happened. Mia tried to call me a bunch of times. She left me a message saying something happened and I needed to call her back. I didn't get it until the next morning, and by then, I couldn't reach her."

Ki was clearly distraught and I was in tears. What had been going through her mind? How angry with me must she have been that she preferred to go to the rec centre by herself than spend the night with me?

"So, I was the reason she wouldn't come back to the house with you?" I felt overcome by guilt. Mia and I had been best friends since we were kids and she was afraid to tell me about Kiowa. I thought of the nights she chose to stay at home when I asked her to stay with me. About that night when she decided to sleep on the riverfront rather than stay at my house. My heart ached for her. Was I so hard to face? Part of me was angry she hid something so huge from me but mostly I felt guilty she felt like she had to.

"So what happened?" I asked.

"I don't know. She didn't say."

"Why didn't she call me again? I would have gone to get her."

"I don't know, Feather. Maybe she thought it was too late?"

"Yeah, she had already woken me up once. You're probably right. But why did they arrest you?" I asked.

"Because I'm the boyfriend. Because I admitted to the police that I saw her that night. Because I don't have an alibi I can prove. Because they need to blame someone and who better than an Aboriginal guy? I don't know, Feather. But I didn't hurt her. I'd never do anything to hurt her, you have to know that," he pleaded. "You've got to help me prove it! I couldn't ask mom . . . she thinks the judge will believe me without any proof."

"What can I do?" I asked him.

"I don't know. Figure out what happened at the rec centre. Figure out a way to prove I dropped her off and she was fine."

"Okay. I will."

"I have to go, Feather. They're calling us for dinner. I'll

talk to you soon, okay?" he said.

"Yeah. Okay." He hung up before I could say anything else.

"Love you," I murmured to the dead phone. As I stared at the photo on my phone, another wave of guilt washed over me. Me, Jake and Mia. If I hadn't pushed her so hard . . . if I had listened when she tried to tell me her mother wouldn't understand like mine would . . . she'd still be here. And I'd have a chance to make it up to her. I was desperate to get that chance.

I reached over to my desk and pulled the crumpled receipt out of my bag. I looked at my list of suspects. He may not have an alibi, but I knew my brother didn't hurt Mia. I stared at his name and then slowly drew a line through it.

CHAPTER 28
CLOSED DOOR

I stared at my phone for days, willing it to ring. Between Mia and Michael, I was basically a slave to my cell phone. When it finally rang, I almost jumped out of my skin.

I fumbled with the phone, dropping it and barely managing to grab it before it hit the floor. "Yeah! Hi!" I was talking very loudly. I took a deep breath. "Sorry. Hello?"

"Feather?" a disembodied voice asked.

"Who's this?" I asked.

"Hi, it's Michael. From the rec centre?" I felt as if my heart stopped beating for a second, then it started galloping like a horse again.

"Michael! Hi."

"Hi. Have you heard from Mia?" he asked.

"No. Nothing yet. Has your guy called you back?"

"Yeah, that's why I'm calling. I finally talked to Larry," he said.

"And?" I couldn't help being impatient with him.

"And he said Mia was at the rec centre that night."

"I knew it! So where is she?" I demanded. "Did he say anything about where she went the next day?"

"That's just it . . . she didn't stay," he told me.

"What do you mean?" I asked. "You said she was there."

"She was. She used the emergency number but Larry didn't hear it for some reason. He says he was doing rounds, but I don't know, maybe he was asleep." My lack of response must have clued him in to my growing anger and he quickly continued. "I'm looking into it, Feather. I obviously can't have someone unreliable working for me."

"Anyway," I prompted.

"Right. So he didn't check the voicemail until the next morning and he heard a message that she had left the night before."

Oh God. "What did it say?" I asked evenly.

He paused for a second before answering.

"That she needed a place to stay for the night, that she'd try again in a while or go down under the Midtown Bridge by the river."

"And did she try again?" I asked.

He sighed.

"Yeah, she left two more messages. Larry didn't get either of those calls. The last time she said she was going to crash under the bridge."

"So with Aboriginal girls going missing all over the city, my friend had to sleep under a bridge like a homeless person?" I asked, outraged. Poor Mia. Why didn't she call me back? I couldn't understand why she chose to sleep on the cold concrete under a bridge where she knew Carli had died, when she could have come back to my house. Was she that angry? Was I really such a horrible friend?

"I'm sorry, Feather. I really am. If Larry did something wrong, I'll find out and fire him immediately. But it's possible it was an honest mistake."

"A mistake that may have gotten her killed!" I shouted at him.

"Don't say that. We have to believe she's still out there somewhere," he said.

"I'm trying!" I answered. "But I can't find her! And she was there, Michael. It proves my brother dropped her off that night! So he couldn't have done something to her. You have to tell the police! You have to tell them it wasn't him. She would have been safe if Larry had let her in." I shook my head in frustration.

"I know. I'm so sorry. All I can do is confirm she was outside the centre that night. I don't know for sure where she went after that." He paused. "And I don't know who she was with when she left."

"What are you talking about?" I asked him, frowning.

"I can't tell the police your brother wasn't still with her after she left, Feather."

"What do you mean? Of course he left! First, he told me he left as soon as she got to the door. It's killing him that he didn't stay until she made it safely inside the centre. And second, she said she'd go down to the bridge. She obviously wouldn't have had to do that if he was still there with her."

"I hear you, Feather. I do," he placated me. "I've met Kiowa. I've seen him with Mia and I don't believe for a second that he would ever hurt her. But I can't swear to that. I can't swear it was him who dropped her off. And if it was, I can't swear he left her there. I'm so incredibly sorry, Feather. I wish I could do more."

"I know. I get it. Thanks for calling, Michael." I hung up and stared at my phone. The background picture was one from last summer when a bunch of us had spent the day at the beach. Sunscreen and sand covered Jake, Mia and me. We had built a towering sandcastle and we stood in front of it, arms around one another with giant grins on our faces. It had been one of the best days of my life. I smiled despite myself but my happiness faded almost immediately. There was one spot in this city Mia could have found a safe place that night, and they turned her away. I pictured Mia walking down to the river from the rec centre, catching the eye of some crazy lunatic who followed her and grabbed her as soon as her guard was down. What if someone had her tied up in his basement right now, crying for me? Or Kiowa?

I looked at my suspect list again and scribbled a giant question mark at the top of the page.

× × ×

There was no possible way to prepare myself for the gossip feeding frenzy that is my high school.

With Ben officially off the hook for Carli's death, which the police were convinced was a suicide, and with Matt out of the closet, the school needed something new to gossip about. The sharks were circling, looking for fresh meat, and I walked right into the belly of the beast.

Jake had an early lacrosse practice, so I made my own way to school. A naive part of me felt that I could get to my classes without anyone paying attention to me. I had flown under the radar for years, so I was surprised when every head in the school turned to stare at me. I didn't think so many people knew who I was.

"That's her!" I heard someone whisper.

"Do you think she helped him kill Mia?" someone else

asked. My face burned. I could feel the heat rising from my neck. Why were they talking about Mia as if she was dead? Why did *everyone* think she was dead? I bit back a reply and kept walking down the hall.

"That girl got what she deserved. She was trouble and her boyfriend is just another stupid Indian who probably got drunk and beat her to death."

I stopped and looked at the girl who said that. I moved into her personal space until I was sure I had her attention.

"What did you just say?" I asked her, my voice low and even.

"I'm sorry, do I know you?" she asked in one of those snotty voices all popular girls at my school seemed to have. She tossed her hair and looked down at the phone in her hand, completely bored by me.

"No, you don't know me," I told her. "But you seem to think you know my brother. You know? The stupid Indian?" I took another step so I was right in her face, forcing her to look up and acknowledge me.

"I don't know what you're talking about," she said. She took a step away from me and hit the wall with her back. She looked at her friends who had suddenly found other things to occupy their attention.

"I think you do. Because you also seem to know my best friend. The girl who got what she deserved?" I took another step forward. She was at least six inches taller than me, but my people? We don't back down. And we can look scary as hell when we want to. "I think you need to be very careful about saying things you know absolutely nothing about. Do you understand?"

She nodded. "Yes," she squeaked.

"Now, I know you're going to start talking about me when I walk away. You'll probably start talking about my brother and my friend again too. But I shouldn't have to listen to your vapid comments."

I started to turn and walk away when I saw her open her mouth to say something to her friends.

"And just so you get it right? My name is Feather." Her mouth snapped shut again and it stayed that way as I left.

I got to the end of the hall without another encounter like that one. I thought maybe the worst had passed when Matt nearly knocked me down.

"Feather! Hey! Can you come with me to the library for a second? There's a really cool book I want to show you," he said, grabbing my hand and pulling me backwards.

"Ummm, yeah. Sure. But can I drop my books off first? Jake said he'd meet me at my locker." I extricated myself from his iron grip and started towards my locker again.

"Oh! He's not there. I think he might be . . . in the library!" Matt grabbed for my hand again. He managed to snag my backpack and drag me backwards.

"Matt! What the hell?" I tried to pull away from him but he was holding on tightly. "What are you doing? Let go!"

"I'm sorry, Feather." He let go but blocked me. Matt's a football player, so when he blocked me, I couldn't even see around him. "Ben made me swear I'd distract you from going to your locker." I could tell by his face that whatever they were trying to keep from me wasn't good.

"What is it, Matt? What am I not supposed to see?" I asked him. He avoided meeting my eyes. I stood on my toes and weaved around in front of him. "Matt! Tell me!"

He sighed deeply. "I can't. Jake will kill me."

"I'm willing to risk it," I muttered and ducked under Matt's arm, bolting down the hall towards my locker. I skidded to a stop when I saw Jake and Ben.

"Feather . . ." Jake began.

"I'm so sorry, man. I tried to stop her. That girl is fast!" Matt pushed his hair off his face and clapped a hand on Jake's shoulder.

"Dude! Could you keep your faggot hands off me?" Jake pushed off Matt's hand. Matt's face registered shock, then hurt. I stared at Jake with my mouth open.

"Jake!" He glanced over at me as I put an arm around Matt. Ben stood still, looking between us silently. "Don't talk to him like that!"

"It's okay, Feather," Matt said.

"No! It's not. It's . . ." I trailed off as I realized Jake had a bunch of crumpled papers in his hands. I looked over at Ben, who was holding a similar handful. Then I looked around the hallway, taking it all in. Jake and Ben had been tearing down photocopies of Kiowa's grad photo someone had enlarged from the yearbook and printed. There had to be a hundred of them plastered on the lockers.

Someone had scrawled "KILLER" in red marker across his face in every single one.

CHAPTER 29
VIGIL

There was a piece of pink paper underneath my windshield wiper when I walked out to my car after school. Another restaurant menu or flyer from a psychic, I thought. I leaned over and pulled it free, crumpling it into a ball just as I registered the faces looking back at me from the bubble-gum pink sheet. I unfurled the ball of paper and bent over, smoothing the wrinkles out against my thigh.

CANDLELIGHT VIGIL

Tonight at the Rec Centre
8:00 pm

Light a candle to show our Stolen Sisters
that we haven't forgotten them.

Light a candle for Carli Thomas — we will never forget you

Light a candle for Mia Joseph — we won't stop looking until we find you

I stared at Mia and Carli looking out at me and ran my

fingers lightly across Mia's face. I missed her so much it hurt.

"Where are you?" I whispered. My phone rang in my pocket. I took it out. Jake. I answered the call but didn't say anything.

"Feather? Listen, please don't say anything. I know you're upset with me. I already apologized to Matt. I don't know why it bothers me that he's gay. But it does. I'm trying, Feather."

"Try harder," I told him. "He's got enough people being hateful to him. You were friends."

"I know," he said. "I really am trying. I just don't get it. How can he like guys? It's disgusting."

"Because he's gay!" I shouted into the phone. "He can't change who he is. And people like you are the reason gay kids kill themselves. Figure it out, Jake. Because Matt's my friend."

"I know he is. I'm sorry." He took a deep breath, pausing before he changed the subject. "Did you get a poster for the vigil on your car?" he asked.

I sighed. "Yeah. It's tonight, right?"

"Can we go together?" He waited for me to answer. "Feather?"

"Jake, I don't know. Everyone will talk if I show up."

"Let them! You have as much right to be there for Mia and Carli as anyone else," he told me.

"I know that! And I feel as if I owe it to Mia, Jake." I paused. "I feel like I wasn't there for her. I should never have taken no for an answer. I should have gone and picked her up. She'd still be here if I hadn't just left her."

"She had Kiowa, Feather." We had an awkward pause after that.

"Yeah. I know. I think I need to do this."

"Me too. And if you're not too pissed off at me, I'll take

you. I'll get Ben to come with us. Matt too," he added.

"Okay. Pick me up after dinner." I hung up without saying goodbye. I pulled out my list of suspects and drew a star beside my boyfriend's name. No matter how hard I wanted to deny it, something about Jake was off. As much as I wished that I could cross him off the list, I just couldn't.

× × ×

There was a huge crowd spilling onto the street outside the rec centre at 7:45. We had parked blocks away and walked over, Jake holding my hand tightly with Matt and Ben flanking us like bodyguards. People gathered in groups, holding candles with Dixie cups shielding their flames from the breeze. Some were holding posters and signs with pictures of lost loved ones. So many women gone. How did this happen?

Michael was standing outside the rec centre, handing out candles and thanking people for coming. I headed over to him, my entourage in tow. He looked up as we approached.

"Feather! I'm glad you came. Listen," he said as he put a hand on my shoulder and leaned down so his words were more private. "Mia brought your brother in a few times and I know he couldn't have had anything to do with her disappearance. I'm sorry for your troubles." He extended a candle to me. I took it, nodding my thanks.

"Têniki. I appreciate that, Michael." He smiled at my thanks and handed candles to Jake and Ben, greeting them both by name. "And this is our friend, Matt." Matt took a candle.

"Nice to meet you, Matt. Thanks for coming. You're all very welcome here." He nodded towards the people still waiting patiently for candles. "You'll excuse me, I hope." We turned and headed back into the throng of people.

I felt a tap on my shoulder as we made our way through the crowd. I turned. A man I didn't recognize stood there smiling at me. I called out for the guys to wait for me.

"Yes?" I asked the man.

"You're Mia's friend, right?" he asked.

"Yeah. We all are." I gestured towards Jake, Ben and Matt. He nodded a greeting at them.

"I'm Larry Kent. I work here at the centre. I wanted to say how sorry I am for what happened to your friend. I assure you I wasn't asleep on the job that night. There was a fight I had to break up and then resolve and I missed your friend's calls. I'm so terribly sorry. We all loved . . . love Mia at the centre." He held out his hand to me. He looked truly miserable and so sincere that I shook his hand. He smiled gratefully at me and reached out to shake each of the boys' hands in turn.

"Thanks for understanding," he said. "I appreciate your kindness."

"Larry!" someone called out. A look of annoyance clouded his face for a second.

"Please excuse me. And thank you again. I'm so glad I got the opportunity to apologize to you. Please let me know if there's anything I can do." He hurried away and I turned back to the guys, who led me towards the front of the crowd.

A platform was set up with a podium and I saw Mia's mother and stepfather standing off to the side. They were sharing a cigarette and laughing at something. I wanted to punch both of them.

"What the hell are they doing here?" I muttered.

By the time Michael walked onto the stage to announce

them and they made their way up the steps to the podium, the smiles had slid right off their faces and they were suddenly teary-eyed and serious.

"I'd like to introduce you to the parents of our missing friend, Mia Joseph. Ladies and gentlemen, please welcome Mr. and Mrs. Miller." He hugged Mia's mother, who was clutching a Kleenex tightly in her fist, then he shook Leonard's hand.

"Thank you for coming. Mia and I have always been close. More like sisters than mother and daughter," her mother said. Unbelievable! "My husband treated Mia like his own daughter and it broke our hearts when she decided to sneak out in the middle of the night to see her boyfriend."

"Is she serious?" I practically yelled into Jake's ear. "Her fantastic husband was groping Mia and she kicked her out!"

"I know, Feather." Jake stroked my arm. I fought the urge to pull away from him as Joyce continued.

"That boyfriend betrayed her trust and took our Mia away from us! We just want our baby back!" Mia's mother sobbed into her hankie. Leonard put his arm around her and led her off the podium. Their feet had barely touched down onto the ground when they were both lighting cigarettes and smiling again. Joyce screeched with laughter at something Leonard said.

"Goddamned phonies!" I hissed. "Ki had nothing to do with this."

"Shhh!" Matt grabbed my arm. "Come on, Feather. We're flying under the radar here. Can you please not attract attention?"

I yanked my arm out of his grasp.

"I'm sorry. But I can't stand it!" I knew my voice was rising but I couldn't help it. My candle was shaking hard in my hand.

"Why don't they tell everyone what really happened?" I glared at Mia's mom, who happened to look up at that moment. She met my eyes and I watched as the colour drained from her face. She leaned over and whispered into Leonard's ear. He glanced up at me, then leaned down and whispered something back.

"Oh shit," Ben said, watching as Joyce and Leonard started walking towards us. "Oh shit. There's no way they just want to say hi, is there?" he asked.

"Probably not," I told him. Matt put a protective arm around me just as they approached us. Joyce walked straight up to me, her chest touching mine.

"What the hell do you think you're doing here?" she glared at me.

"I'm here for Mia and Carli," I told her, taking a step away from the overpowering stench of cigarettes and dollar-store perfume. "That's all. I'm not trying to cause any problems, Joyce." I held my hands up in front of me, before realizing it looked like I was proving I didn't have a weapon. I put them back down. Joyce flinched anyway, then looked around to see if anyone was watching.

"How dare you!" she screamed, her face turning an alarming shade of eggplant. Or maybe it was puce. Wait. Was puce purple? I was internally debating her colour palette when she hauled off and slapped me, hard, across the face. I staggered back, right into Jake, who grabbed me before I could fall. My face was on fire, both from the humiliation and from the pain of the attack.

"Hey!" Jake yelled. "Get away from her!" Matt and Ben stepped forward, blocking me from further attack, but Joyce was in full-on freak-out mode.

"Why are you doing this to me?" she shrieked. "My daughter is missing! She's probably dead. And your brother took her!" I opened my mouth to respond but she cut me off. "You have the nerve to come here and put me through having to see you when it was your brother who killed my daughter!"

"What the hell are you talking about?" I pushed past the boys and stood in front of Joyce. "Kiowa didn't do anything, Joyce. He picked Mia up after you kicked her out of the house in the middle of the night when you didn't want to face the awful truth! That your husband is a creepy pervert who tried to have sex with her."

I heard gasps from the people who had gathered to watch us go at it. She started to talk but it was my turn. "And don't even think of denying it to me, Joyce, because I saw it with my own eyes. Isn't that right, Leonard?" Leonard looked like he hoped the ground might open up and swallow him so he could disappear. "You both make me sick." I turned to walk away and then spun back around. "And Mia is NOT dead, Joyce. What kind of mother gives up on her own daughter?" I turned my back on them and stalked away. Matt, Jake and Ben followed close behind.

"So much for flying below the radar," Matt said to Ben.

"Hey!" a voice called out behind us. "Feather!" I turned and saw Michael pushing through the crowd towards us.

"This can't be good," I whispered to no one in particular.

"Hold up, guys," Michael said, jogging up to us. "Feather, was all of that true? What you just said to them?" He nodded towards Joyce and Leonard, who were huddled together, passing a cigarette back and forth between them. I sighed.

"Yeah, Michael. It is. I know we didn't tell you what was really going on. I'm sorry. But hey, Joyce always did want to be on TV." I gestured to the news cameras. "She wanted to be a weather girl, but I'm sure this is more than enough attention for her."

"Feather, let it go," Jake warned, glancing towards Leonard and Joyce. I doubted that she'd dare attack me again but he was right. I didn't need to draw any more attention to myself.

"I didn't know. I never would have asked them to speak here." He rubbed his chin. "I knew Mia had problems with her parents but all of the kids here do. Shit. I need to get back up there and say something. I'm sorry for . . . that." He gestured at me. "Is your face okay?" He gave me a half smile.

"Yeah." I felt my cheek. It was a little sore and maybe swollen but I'd be fine. "I'll live," I told him.

"I appreciate you coming. All of you." He smiled at us and waved as he loped back up to the podium and addressed the crowd. "Thank you everyone for coming out to show your support for our missing and murdered loved ones. Let's talk about how we can stay safe," he began.

"I've heard enough," I told the guys. "Can we just get out of here?"

"Yes!" All three of them shouted back at me.

"Okay, okay." I grabbed Matt's hand and threw an arm around Ben, who clapped Jake into a headlock. "Let's go back to my place and order a pizza."

× × ×

I left the guys in front of the TV, inhaling the pizza. My list was on my desk where I left it. I sat down and stared at the suspects, then slowly crossed off Ben's name. Anyone could have taken Carli and Mia but I didn't believe it was Ben. His grief at losing Carli was definitely genuine. And Mia had shown him nothing but friendship. He had no reason to hurt her. It couldn't be him. I stared down at Jake's name and put the receipt in my desk drawer without crossing it out.

CHAPTER 30
SUGAR'S SWEET, SO IS SHE

He watched her stalking through the crowd. So many people. So many women! But he only had eyes for her. She stood out. She shone. He watched her stand up to the parents. He watched her take a slap like a man and he felt himself get hard. He put his hand in his pocket and rubbed himself, not caring if anyone saw him or not.

She was perfection. Flawless.

Her skin was bronzed. Her hair was black as a raven's wing. Her eyes were like dark chocolate.

Eyes that you could get lost in.

Her lips were full and red. Like a ripe strawberry.

He throbbed.

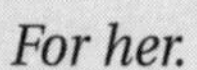

For her.

She brushed against him and he leaned forward slightly to breathe in the scent of her green apple shampoo.

He had never wanted anyone as much as he wanted her.

He watched her walk away from him and wanted more than anything to reach out and run his hand down the bare skin of her arm.

It was only a matter of time.

CHAPTER 31
JUST ANOTHER NUMBER

I hadn't seen the television cameras on me when I was arguing with Mia's mom. But there I was in glorious HD, eyes flashing and jaw clenched as I yelled and confronted her for kicking out Mia. I cringed. My mother was going to kill me.

I switched channels and there I was again. *I am so dead when my mom gets home,* I thought. I instantly regretted my choice of words, even if they were just in my head.

I turned the TV off and went to do the dishes. I figured my mom coming home to some random acts of housework charity might ease the blow of seeing her daughter getting into a screaming match on national television.

The dishes turned into vacuuming and then dusting. By the time I was done, the house was spotless and I was exhausted. I grabbed a carton of Chocolate Peanut Butter Häagen-Dazs, picked up a spoon from the drying rack and flopped back on the couch with a sigh of contentment. I had just dug my spoon into the carton and was licking it clean when my phone rang. I tried to swallow the huge lump of peanut butter that was sticking to the roof of my mouth.

"Ugh . . . 'ello?" I was scraping at it with my tongue, trying to swallow so I could talk.

"Hello? Is this Feather Bedard?" a strange, male voice asked.

I swallowed hard, finally clearing the peanut butter and wishing I had a glass of milk.

"Yes it is. Who is this?"

"You don't know me," the man said rather ominously. "But I got your number from Michael at the rec centre?" That was at least a little reassuring. "He thought we should talk."

"Okay," I ventured. "About what, exactly?"

"Oh, I'm sorry. I should start at the beginning. My name is Paul Abenaki." He paused for a second, apparently to gather his thoughts, because he dove right back in. "My girlfriend, Sara, died last year."

"I'm so sorry," I began, not sure how to respond. A total stranger calls me out of the blue . . . this was just getting weirder and weirder.

"Thanks. Michael thought I should call you because she died down by the Riverwalk. Near the Midtown Bridge?"

My heart stopped.

"Are you still there?" he asked.

"Yeah." I swallowed. "Sorry. So what happened, Paul?" I couldn't believe what I was hearing. How long had this been going on?

"They found her under the overpass. They said it was an accident and she had somehow fallen."

"But you don't think she fell," I said. It wasn't a question.

"No, Feather," he replied sourly. "I know she didn't."

"How do you know?" I asked. I thought about Ben's

confidence that Carli hadn't killed herself and Kiowa denying he had anything to do with Mia's disappearance.

"Because I was on the phone with her when it happened. Someone came up to her and said something. I could hear his voice but I couldn't make out what he said to her. Sara must have known him. She said hi and asked how he was . . . then she said no to him . . . then she screamed, 'no and please . . .'" Paul's voice broke. "And she called my name. Her phone went dead after that." He paused and took a deep, shaking breath. "She called my name and I couldn't help her."

"Oh my God . . . Tom, I'm so, so sorry. Did the police look for her right away?"

"I was close by so I sped over to the bridge but she wasn't there. I walked all around it. I walked under it. No one was there. I called the police but they didn't find any sign of her."

"But I thought you said she fell?" I asked, perplexed.

"That's just it. She wasn't there. I looked everywhere. The police looked everywhere. She was gone. I told them what had happened — that someone was there with her but they didn't believe me. They said it was just 'the ramblings of a hysterical boyfriend.' I had been drinking," he said quietly. "Just a couple of beers but they said I was drunk and didn't know what I was saying."

"So when did they find her?" I asked.

"They found her the next day. A jogger found her under the bridge." His voice was shaking.

"Somewhere you didn't look?" I asked.

"No. Exactly where I looked the day before. Also where the police looked. I had been standing in the exact spot she was found," he told me, his voice bitter.

"But how is that possible? What did the police say?" I demanded.

"They said they must have missed her the day before."

"But you're sure you didn't," I said.

"I know I didn't. There was a graffiti heart right above where they found her. I saw it when I was looking for her."

"Wow. I can't believe this," I said.

He sighed.

"I don't know, Feather. Apparently, I wasn't a reliable witness in my 'drunken stupor.' The medical examiner said she died of blunt force trauma consistent with a fall. They ignored the fact that I heard someone attack her. They ignored the fact that her body wasn't there the night before. It's like they didn't want to bother investigating. They just closed the case. Just another dead Indian girl."

"I'm sorry, Paul. How can the police not see the obvious? Someone is taking these girls! Sara, my friend Carli and now my best friend, Mia. All of them were down by the water near that overpass. They called Carli a suicide. Your girlfriend fell accidentally. And Mia is still missing."

"I'm not helping much, but I wanted you to know your friends aren't the only girls who went missing down there. Someone is targeting Indigenous women," he said. "And the police don't care about finding whoever is doing this."

"You're right. They're completely ignoring the connection between what's happening to these girls."

"I'm sorry about that. If there's anything I can do or if you decide to search or need something from me, just ask. I couldn't help Sara but maybe I can help you."

I thanked him and hung up. Why didn't more people care about these women? There was something going on down by the riverfront, and if no one else was willing to investigate, I was going to take matters into my own hands. But before I tried to find out who was really responsible, I had to clear my brother's name. And to do that, I had to go see him.

CHAPTER 32
THE WRC

The drive up to the Winnipeg Remand Centre was quiet. Jake hummed along to the radio, glancing over at me occasionally.

"Are you okay?" he asked me for the hundredth time.

"Yep. Still okay," I told him, trying to smile as the WRC came into view.

The sight of the futuristic, imposing glass building made my skin crawl. I hated the idea of my smart, sensitive, smiling brother trapped in there.

Jake parked in the lot and turned to me, his hand resting on my thigh. I shifted in my seat, causing his hand to slide off my leg. Jake sighed.

"Do you want me to come in with you?" he asked.

I did. I hated the idea of going in there alone. But I wasn't sure how Kiowa was going to react, so I thought I should probably do this myself. This time anyway.

"No." I sighed. "But thanks. I appreciate the offer." He leaned over and kissed me on the cheek.

"If you're not back in an hour, I'll come in, guns blazing," he promised.

"You're a dork," I told him, softening slightly towards him. I leaned in and kissed the smirk off his soft mouth. I sighed again. This constant back and forth between being the perfect boyfriend and angry homophobe was exhausting. There was something scary about his extreme mood swings. I didn't know what to do. "Okay. I better go in."

He nodded and I took my time unbuckling my seatbelt and easing open the door. I slung my purse over my shoulder and set off towards the entrance of the WRC.

A security guard buzzed me in and had me sign in and show my ID. He rummaged around in my purse and then walked me into a small room where a woman was sitting at a table, crying, while a guy in an orange jumpsuit looked blankly at the wall behind her. At another table, an inmate was laughing with an older man who looked so much like him; it could only be his father. They looked like they frequented the same tattoo parlour. Well, however you choose to bond, I thought.

I sat down at an empty table and stared at my hands clenched in my lap. I willed myself to calm down but my heart was galloping wildly.

A door opened off to the side and my brother entered the room. He wasn't wearing shackles or even handcuffs, so that was good. He was pale, but otherwise, he still looked like Kiowa. I stood up to hug him but he stopped and held up his hands in front of him.

"Sorry, Feather. I'm not allowed to touch you." He smiled sadly at me.

"Oh, right. Right!" I replied, too brightly. Way too brightly. I swallowed and tried again. "You look good, Kiowa."

"Thanks." He smiled, less sadly now. "It's good to see you!"

"You too," I said. "I brought you some stuff to read." Nothing like cutting to the chase — I plunged ahead. "Turns out there have been a bunch of girls who disappeared or died down by the riverfront under really suspicious circumstances."

Kiowa raised his eyebrows as I slid printouts of news stories towards him. He glanced down, frowning and leafing through a couple. "Okay. I'll take a look. But give me the short version."

I filled him in on the details of Sara's case and what Paul had told me. I had dug up information about a couple of other girls as well.

"Wow." He took a deep breath. "Why isn't anyone investigating?"

"I don't know. The RCMP released a report recently. Aboriginal women are disappearing and being killed in record numbers. Remember Mom said that we're four times more likely to be killed than non-Aboriginals?"

"I still can't believe that." Kiowa shook his head.

"I know. The government says the killings and disappearances are isolated events that should be left to the local police forces."

"Of course," he spit out bitterly. "No one cares about a missing Aboriginal girl like Mia." He looked up at me. "No one but us. You know I didn't hurt her, right?" he asked, grabbing my hands.

"No touching, Bedard," the guard called out. Kiowa let go but he didn't break eye contact with me.

"I know you didn't," I assured him.

"Then you have to help me!"

"How?" I asked.

"Is there a sign-in sheet or a video camera at the rec centre?"

I shook my head. "There isn't. I already asked Michael."

"Okay." He looked away, a frown creasing his forehead.

"What about a gas receipt? I filled up near the school. Maybe the gas station has a camera?"

"Maybe." I couldn't help sounding skeptical. "What about a credit card bill?"

"I used cash," he said. "Maybe a camera at the dorm?"

"I can look into it," I told him.

He slammed his hand down on the table, and then glanced over at the guard.

"There has to be something that'll prove I wasn't there! I didn't do this, Feather!"

"I know, Ki. I believe you. I'll find something, okay?"

"Promise me, Feather. I know what they're saying about me out there. Get me out of here so we can find Mia and bring her home."

"I will, Kiowa." I met his eyes. "I promise.

× × ×

Jake was leaning against the car waiting for me when I came out. I still had doubts, but I needed the perfect boyfriend at that moment. I walked up to him and threw my arms around his neck, holding him tightly. I closed my eyes and breathed in the scent of him. He kissed the top of my head and held me back, waiting for me to speak.

I drew a shaky breath and let him go.

"I'm okay," I told him. "I have to figure out a way to get Kiowa out of there."

He nodded, and then opened the door for me. He walked around to the other side and got behind the wheel. He ran a hand through his hair. It was getting even blonder from the time he spent outside playing lacrosse and working on his car.

"How did it go?" he asked. "Is Kiowa okay?"

"Yeah. He is. But he's scared. He wants me to find something that will clear his name and get him out of there."

"I'll help," he said.

"Thanks. I just need to figure out where to start." I looked at him, so eager to help me clear Kiowa's name. How could he be so nice and hide that ugly side of himself so easily? The more it happened, the more unease I felt around him, but I needed all the help I could get.

"What did he suggest?" he asked.

"He wrote down where he filled his tank with gas near his school. Maybe they have a security camera?"

Jake nodded. "Okay. What else?"

"Security at the school."

"So we'll drive down and take a look around, talk to some people and see what we can find out," he suggested.

"Yeah. I'm in."

"It's a good start," he said.

I nodded but I already knew where I had to start. If someone was taking Aboriginal girls from the riverfront, I needed to go down there myself. If the police weren't willing to scout out the river, then I would.

CHAPTER 33
GOING UNDER COVER

There was not one thing in my closet that didn't scream "I shop at the Gap!" Most of my wardrobe consisted of T-shirts with superheroes on them, jeans and yoga pants — nothing I could imagine wearing to the riverfront on a hunt for whoever took Mia.

My eyes pricked with tears. After this much time, I still refused to consider that I might never see my best friend again. If the police were going to throw my brother in jail when there was no way he had anything to do with Mia's disappearance, then I'd have to look for the guy myself. I felt anger rising up in me again like a wave of nausea I couldn't swallow. Why did at least three girls going missing from the same place not set off any alarms? I sighed, pushing clothes hangers across the rod, crashing them together and sending a pair of khaki capris to the floor. I bent down to retrieve them and stopped as my gaze fell on an unfamiliar backpack lying on the floor. I reached for it, and then paused, realizing who it belonged to. Mia.

I picked it up, trying to remember when Mia had put it there. I drew a blank. It was heavy in my hands, bulging at the seams. Mia had sketched and written all over it. I ran my hand over a realistic drawing of her dog, JayJay, and smiled. My fingers stopped at a tiny red heart by the clasp. I squinted at it, and then recognized a minuscule 'K' written in tiny script. How had I not known? I shook my head and pushed the ever-present guilt down as I opened Mia's bag. Clothes spilled out onto the bedroom floor. Shirts, pants, a jacket, skirts . . . an entire wardrobe. It was as if she thought she might need to take off suddenly and stay away for a while. I sighed and started picking up the clothes.

I was folding a silver miniskirt with black skulls printed on it when it occurred to me that if I was going to the riverfront to attract a killer, I'd need a disguise. Mia's clothes were exactly what I needed to go under cover and not look so much like I was about to bust out some choreography from an Old Navy commercial.

I laid her miniskirt on the bed and looked over the rest of Mia's clothes. I picked up a black tank top and placed it on the bed with the skirt. I had a sudden flash of inspiration that led me first to my dresser, where I had a pair of fishnet stockings left over from Halloween, then towards the basement door.

I flicked the switch as I started down the stairs. My mom had spent a lot of money fixing up the basement so she and Kiowa could watch the Jets and he could play his video games. I rarely went down there unless I had to find something in the storage room. Piled floor to ceiling with cardboard boxes and plastic bins, the storage room was tidy but unorganized. Boxes labelled "kitchen" were nestled on top of a bin inexplicably marked "boxes" and another with a "tools" label. I stood in the centre of the room, hands on my hips, and looked around. "Kiowa's lacrosse trophies" was on top of "Feather's sculptures" — from my ill-fated foray into art classes with

Mia — and "Feather's shoes and junk" in my own handwriting. I pulled Kiowa's box of trophies down and stood on my toes to lift the plastic lid off my shoe bin. I fished around, pulling out my junior high cheerleading sweater (a social experiment engineered by Mia), and a stuffed elephant I had creatively named Ellie. I reached in further, spotting a flash of cherry red, and pulled out my old Doc Martens. I hadn't worn them in years but they'd go great with my outfit. Mia's outfit, I amended. To find the guy who took my friend, I'd have to become Mia. At least for a little while.

I stood in front of the mirror and stared at my reflection critically. I pulled at the hem of Mia's skirt, willing it to lengthen another couple of inches. I wasn't entirely convinced that my ass wasn't showing. The tank top showed off cleavage made impressive with the help of a push-up bra. The red Docs definitely made the outfit, though. I turned, twisting my head, trying in vain to tell if anyone really could see my ass. I didn't think so . . . as long as I didn't bend over.

I turned back around and leaned in towards the mirror, running my fingertips under my eyes and smudging the coal-black eyeliner I had found with the Halloween fishnets. That would have to do. This was as close to psycho bait as I was going to get.

The next step was less clear. I figured I'd hang out at the riverfront because that's where Mia, Carli and Sara all went missing. I had no idea if they met the guy down there or not. They could have caught his attention anywhere. I wasn't even sure what I'd do if I found him. I hadn't thought that far ahead. But I had to start somewhere.

I sighed, wishing I could call Jake and get him to come with me for backup. But there was no way he would agree to putting me in danger. And truthfully, I wasn't sure I really wanted him there. Standing in my bedroom, surrounded by all my pictures of me and Mia, I felt completely alone.

× × ×

I hadn't been down to the river at night before. It was completely different when it was dark. During the day, the Riverwalk was populated with young moms with jogging strollers and tourists with cameras slung around their necks. Couples strolled hand-in-hand along the riverbank on romantic dates. It was a safe place to walk and get some nice views of the city during the day.

But at night, the riverfront came alive with street kids, homeless people, people looking to score drugs and sex workers looking for dates. I felt completely out of place until I remembered that I was in disguise. I walked past a group of kids about my own age, passing a joint back and forth. They nodded at me as I walked by, maybe thinking they knew me from some other night below the overpass.

As I walked towards the bridge, I looked at each person I passed, hoping one would be Mia. It never was. But the sheer number of Aboriginal girls hanging out alone or just with one other girl was mind-boggling. Didn't they know how dangerous it was for them? Hadn't they read the statistics? I wanted to yell, "Get out of here! We're four times more likely to be killed than that white girl over there!" But I didn't.

I saw places where the street lights didn't penetrate the darkness. I was afraid to look too closely after hearing some of the moaning sounds coming from the darkness. There were too many places where someone could hide. Could watch.

Could reach out and grab. Far too many places where someone could drag a girl and make it sound like they were on a "date."

I was so deep in thought I didn't notice I had walked away from the groups of people. Aside from the odd pedestrian hurrying past in the other direction, I was alone. The gloomy spots on the Riverwalk seemed even darker where there were no people, no voices.

I jumped at a shadow and started moving faster, the overpass looming ahead of me. It was even darker there. The lights didn't reach very far. The space underneath was black velvet, cloaking everything. I could make out nothing but shadows. I stepped into the suffocating darkness.

I heard a scraping sound to my right. I jumped and tried to see what it was, but what little light was there played tricks with my eyes and cast murky shapes on the walls. I thought I heard footsteps but they could have come from anywhere. A sound like a sigh came from behind me. I held my breath and turned slowly. I thought I saw something move.

"Is someone there?" I asked, willing my voice to sound steady. "Hello?" I waited, holding my breath, but there was no response. I let out a breath and turned again, walking with my arms held out in front of me. Shadows danced around me, and what could have been a rat skittered around my foot. I squealed and kicked but missed it.

I stopped again and heard someone draw a deep breath right behind me. I ran a few steps forward and turned, fists swinging but touching only air.

"Who's there?" I demanded, feeling considerably less brave then I had when I walked in. I stood still. Waiting. I tried to see around me but I could only make out vague shapes. I wasn't even sure which way led out to the Riverwalk, I was so disoriented. I was about to try to trace my steps back out when someone blew softly into my ear.

I screamed and swung my arm with all my might, catching whoever it was . . . a man from his grunt of pain . . . in what I took to be his face. I ran, guessing wildly which way was out. He reached out and grabbed my arm but I shook him loose, still screaming. I was back out on the Riverwalk with a few more steps. I ran until I was standing under a street light, the voices of a group of kids talking about music filling my ears. Then I turned and looked behind me. A man was standing just at the edge of the darkness under the bridge, watching me. His features were hidden. I stared, breathing hard, backing away slowly towards the voices behind me. There was something vaguely familiar about him but I couldn't put my finger on it. I turned and walked towards the sound, the light. I stopped a couple of feet away from the kids and turned back once more to see if he was still there.

As I watched, he raised a hand at me and waved.

CHAPTER 34
INTO THE LIGHT OF THE DARK BLACK NIGHT

Even if he hadn't recognized her, the scent of her green apple shampoo would have told him this was his girl. How lucky that he didn't even have to go looking for her. Of all the bridges in all the world, she had to walk under his.

God, she was beautiful. There was a fire to her, an energy he rarely found in women. He'd been under the bridge long enough to allow his eyes to adjust to the murky dimness, but hers hadn't, and she was inching along with her arms held out in front of her. He longed to touch her but he settled for watching. He was good at that.

He stepped closer, breathing in her scent. She heard him and started punching at the air. She was glorious. So much fight in her.

He liked that.

He toyed with her, like a cat toys with a mouse before pouncing. He lifted a lock of her hair and smelled it . . . then he blew into her ear.

He was rewarded with an ear-piercing shriek that echoed off the concrete as she swung her arm and hit him. She ran away from him then. He followed to the edge of the shadows and watched her run, her hair bouncing against her back.

He thought about chasing her . . . grabbing her and dragging her back into the soft cover of darkness under the bridge . . . but he paused when he saw the clothes, the dark makeup. She looked like any other slutty Indian girl. He wanted her back the way she looked at the vigil. He could wait.

Besides, he still hadn't gotten rid of the last one yet.

CHAPTER 35
SEARCHING FOR CLUES

My stealthy trip down to the overpass didn't amount to much, but it scared the hell out of me. Whoever that guy was, I firmly believed he wasn't some random homeless person. There was something about the way he had crept up behind me . . . I had an incredibly bad feeling about him. That was *the* guy. I was convinced he had something to do with Carli's murder and Mia's disappearance.

Even though there was something familiar about him, I was no closer to finding out who he was. Unfortunately, I couldn't go into the police station and tell them some random guy on the Riverwalk creeped me out and he's probably a serial killer so they should definitely arrest him. And let my brother out of Remand while you're at it, please.

Later that night, I sat on the sofa beside Jake. I was torn. I knew he'd be upset if I told him I went down to the underpass by myself but I had to tell him about the guy. The feeling I had about him . . . he was the guy . . . there was something to it. It wasn't just in my head.

I cleared my throat.

"Jake?" I was afraid to look up.

"Yeah?" He twisted his head to look at me. I avoided his gaze.

"I have to tell you something," I said. He pulled away from me so he could look into my eyes. I was always a sucker for those blue eyes. I think that might be what made me overlook his obvious character flaws. I told him everything that happened to me on the Riverwalk, holding nothing back. To his credit, he let me talk and didn't interrupt. His face betrayed nothing, even though I knew he was probably pissed off that I went there alone at night. Jake was a master at hiding his emotions.

When I got to the part where the guy waved at me, he finally lost it.

"Feather, what the hell were you thinking? If that's the same guy who took Mia and killed Carli, you could have been next! Why didn't you tell me so I could go with you and make sure you were safe?" He looked more scared than mad, which surprised me. I hadn't expected him to understand, but I didn't think he'd lash out at me either.

"I didn't think you'd let me go if I told you," I admitted.

"Let you?" he asked incredulously. "Since when could I stop you from doing something you wanted to do?" He sighed and reached a hand out, touching my face. "I love you, Feather. If anything happened to you . . ." He trailed off. I was torn. The truth was, I didn't know how I felt about him anymore.

"I know. I'm sorry. I don't even know what I was looking for. Just . . . something. How else could I help Kiowa?"

He thought for a minute, a frown creasing his forehead. Then he reached over and squeezed my hand.

"We try to prove he was at that gas station. We'll see if they have surveillance video and we'll search every inch of his car and dorm room to find that receipt. But next time, Feather? Just ask for my help, okay?" he asked.

God, I couldn't help it. Despite everything, I still loved him.

As I lay in bed that night, I realized it couldn't have been Jake watching me beneath the overpass. First, I knew what his cologne smelled like and this guy smelled . . . off. Like bananas left on the counter too long. And second, Jake was taller and broader than that guy was. I felt guilty I had even suspected him in the first place.

I had no idea who took Mia. Or who killed Carli or Sara. It could have been Paul, who I had never met. It could have been someone at school. It could have been someone they didn't know at all. I was no closer to finding Mia or who took her than I was before going under cover on the Riverwalk. Something the police weren't making a priority was taking up my entire life and I was at a complete loss. I sat up in bed and switched on my lamp. I slid open my desk drawer and took out my list. I looked at it for a minute and then ripped it into tiny pieces.

× × ×

The police had searched Kiowa's car but I assumed they didn't find much because they returned it a few days later. His dorm room had been searched and catalogued. They likely found evidence that Mia had been in the car at the very least and probably in his room, but I was sure there wasn't anything suspicious. I knew my brother.

I knew that Kiowa left his spare keys to both with my mom in case he lost his. I took them off the hook by the front door, knowing I'd get them back before she even noticed they were gone. Kiowa's car was in our driveway so I should have thought to go through it before I wandered down through the seedy riverfront.

Whereas my car was spotless, Kiowa's looked like a hurricane blew through it. Blew through it and tore strips off the upholstery. I was about to point it out to Jake when I realized it was probably the police who had torn up his car. Bastards. They could have at least thrown out the garbage.

I grabbed a plastic bag from the floor of the passenger side and started going through each little shred of paper, looking for a receipt proving he was somewhere else at the same time Mia was calling the rec centre over and over.

"Throw out the trash, okay?" I told Jake, who was in the back seat sorting through the garbage. I had to admit that we couldn't blame the police for the whole mess. Jake nodded and picked up another bag and started stuffing empty Coke cans and fast food wrappers into it.

"Gah!" Jake yelled in the back seat.

"What?" I sat up and looked back at him.

"I just put my hand through a mouldy orange!"

I laughed despite the fact my hands were grubby and I had a strand of hair in my mouth that I was afraid to wipe away for fear of getting a disease from the filth covering my fingers.

"Get back to work," I told him.

It took a good hour to clean up Kiowa's car and read every single piece of paper to see if it could possibly clear him. There was a moment of excitement when Jake found a gas receipt. Until upon closer inspection, we discovered it was from several months earlier.

I went into the house, grabbed a couple of Diet Cokes and went back out, handing one to Jake. We sat on the driveway, leaning against Kiowa's car, sipping our drinks and planning our next move.

"We've got the keys to his dorm room. Let's go there and see if we can find anything," Jake said. I nodded.

"Okay. But if it's anything like his car was, we'll never find the receipt," I grumbled, licking the moisture dripping down the outside of my can before it could hit my hand.

"You don't think it'll be this bad, do you?" he asked. I shrugged.

"Only one way to find out," I told him. He stood up and held a hand out to me, pulling me up with him. He held me against him for a moment. I realized suddenly how long it had been since we were together.

"I miss you," he whispered. He held me tighter, sighing into my hair.

"I know. Me too."

I felt guilty. We were supposed to be helping my brother and here I was, lusting after my boyfriend, the violent homophobe. I pulled away.

"We should probably go," I told him.

After about five minutes of driving, I saw a familiar sign out of the corner of my eye.

"Wait!" I told Jake. "That's the gas station! Turn around!"

Jake pulled a U-turn and drove into the station. He parked and turned the engine off, then glanced over at me.

"Ready?" he asked.

"Let's go," I told him.

The bell over the door dinged as we went in. The

bored-looking cashier peered up from his magazine and idly turned the page. The store was empty otherwise. Jake nudged my arm and nodded towards the surveillance camera behind the counter. Yes! I approached the guy behind the counter. Patrick, his name tag said.

"Excuse me? Hi. Patrick? I was wondering what the protocol was for checking out the surveillance video?" I asked him, putting on what I hoped was my most alluring smile. "Can just anyone look at it, or what?"

"Who are you?" he asked, peering at me as if trying to decide if he actually knew me or if I was just some random customer.

"Feather. Hi." I held out my hand to him. He shook it, still trying to place me. "And this is Jake. So the video?"

"I don't know. No one's ever asked before. I guess it's okay. What day are you looking for?" he asked.

I looked over at Jake triumphantly. We had it! Kiowa would be on that tape and he'd be in the clear. I was already picturing him walking out a free man.

I leaned over the counter and gave him the date.

"Wait, that's more than a week ago," he said.

"Yeah." I glanced at Jake again. What was going on? "Why? What's wrong?"

"We only keep the tapes for a week, then we tape over them. See?" He pointed to a shelf behind him where there were honest-to-God VHS tapes with the days of the week written on them. I felt myself deflate.

"Are you sure everything gets taped over?" Jake asked. "No exceptions?"

Paul looked at him, completely perplexed.

"What kind of exception could there possibly be?"

"I don't know. Maybe you bought new tapes or something?"

Paul laughed.

"Can you even buy these anymore? Nope. We've been using the same tapes as long as I've been working here. If you're looking for footage from more than a week ago, it doesn't exist. Sorry."

"You're sure?" I asked hopelessly.

"Yeah. Sorry. Were you looking for something important?" Paul asked.

"Yeah. Pretty important. Thanks anyway," I said, trying to smile. We turned and started walking towards the door when I had another thought. "One more thing," I said, turning back to the counter. "Do you remember seeing this guy in here?" I held out my phone with a picture of me and Kiowa standing outside the house, smiling goofily.

"Uh . . ." He looked at the picture for a second, then glanced back at me. "The cops came in a while back asking about him. He had something to do with his girlfriend's death?" He looked back at me expectantly.

"She's not dead," I muttered.

"Oh. Okay. Well, I saw him on TV but I don't remember him coming in here before. I told the cops the same thing."

"Did they see the tape?" I asked him.

"Nah. They didn't even ask. We had already erased it by the time they came, anyway." He stopped and looked at me. "You know him?" he asked.

"Yeah," I told him, putting away my phone and turning to leave. "I do."

CHAPTER 36
THE EVIDENCE

Our next stop was nearby at least. I had the keys to get into Kiowa's dorm and no one looked at us twice when we walked into the building. They probably assumed we were students. I hadn't realized it was a co-ed dorm but it was definitely to my advantage now.

"Which room is it?" Jake whispered, glancing at the students as we passed them. They were studying or talking, typing on laptops and reading. No one even noticed us.

I walked a little further and stopped, remembering the number from the birthday card I had addressed and sent to Kiowa earlier this year. We had an ongoing competition to see who could find the cheesiest card.

"This one." I put the key in the lock and turned it.

"Hey! What the hell?" A guy Kiowa's age leapt off the bed — off the girl! — and covered himself with a pillow. The girl screamed and wrapped the sheet around herself while Jake and I stood in the doorway staring, our mouths open in shock.

I tried to look away but it was just too funny. "I'm sorry . . ."

"Get out!" the boy yelled and stepped towards us, causing his pillow to drop a few critical inches. I looked away.

"Uh, you might want to . . ." I gestured at his pillow. He

looked down and clutched it higher against himself.

"How did you get a key to my room?" he asked angrily.

"Isn't this Kiowa Bedard's room?" I asked, backing out of the doorway. The boy held the door open and paused, looking at my face.

"You're his sister, aren't you?" he asked. I looked at him quizzically. "I saw your picture in his room." I nodded. "They took all his stuff out when it didn't look like he'd be back and gave the room to me. I was next on the list."

"Where did they put his stuff?" Jake asked.

"Try the RA," he said. "The Resident Advisor. She's downstairs by the elevator."

"Thanks . . . and sorry about that." Jake and I turned away.

"Hey!" the boy called out. We looked back at him. "Everyone around here likes your brother. We don't believe he did anything. Tell him his dorm mates are thinking about him, okay?"

"Thanks. I will," I promised. I took Jake's hand and went in search of the RA.

Her room was easy to find. There was a big sign on the door, indicating the Resident Advisor was available. Jake knocked, while I prayed she was alone — and had some clothes on. A pleasant-looking, diminutive girl with blue hair in dreadlocks opened the door.

"Hi," she chirped. "Can I help you?" She pulled idly at her hair while she looked us over. "You're not from my dorm," she noted.

"Nope," Jake said.

"I'm Kiowa Bedard's sister. We're looking for the things that were taken out of his room?" I said.

"Hi. Yeah, I've got his stuff. I was going to contact your family but it kind of slipped my mind." She turned away and rummaged around in her disaster of a room. Clothes everywhere. Boxes tipped over on each other. How she found anything in there was beyond me. “Here it is!” she crowed, grabbing a box that seemed way too small to hold all of his stuff.

“That’s all his stuff?” I asked, skeptically.

”I think there’s a suitcase too. It’d be in the storage room. And the cops took a bunch of stuff.”

I reached for the box, but she stepped back.

“Do you have some ID?” she asked. I pulled out my wallet and showed her my driver’s license. “Feather Bedard. Yeah, I remember him talking about you. Sorry about that.” She handed me the box. “I’ll just grab the suitcase.” She darted out of her room, leaving the door ajar.

“Does she even have a bed in there?” Jake asked, eyeing the mess. I shrugged. She reappeared, dragging a big suitcase on wheels behind her.

“Here you go. Tell your brother hi from us, okay?”

“Sure. Thanks,” I said, following Jake and the suitcase out the door.

As soon as we got to the car, I began tearing into the box. Jake opened the suitcase and started looking through it.

“At least someone folded his stuff,” he said. “I’m guessing it wasn’t her.”

We looked through Kiowa’s belongings in silence for a few minutes.

“Shit,” I said. “It’s not here, Jake.” I looked over at him hopefully. He shook his head.

“Just clothes,” he said.

“Damn it!” I slammed a book back into the box and stood up. “We know he didn’t do it! Why can’t we find something to prove it?” Jake pulled me into his arms and kissed my head.

"We'll find something, Feather. We just have to keep looking." He opened the car door for me and then walked back to the trunk to put Kiowa's stuff inside.

× × ×

"Holy shit!" Jake yelled, stomping on the brake and turning the wheel sharply to the right. He pulled off to the side of the road, staring out the window at something in the distance.

"What?" I asked, my heart pounding, one hand still on the dashboard to brace myself.

He pointed and I asked, "What am I supposed to be looking at, Jake?"

"The cell tower!" he shouted excitedly.

"Huh?" I still wasn't getting his point. And I was losing patience. It had been a rotten day and I was ready to go home and soak in the bath for an hour with a good book.

"Feather!" He turned towards me, a smile on his face. "If Kiowa had his location service turned on, his phone will show where he was that night! It'll pinpoint his location and tell us what time he was there!"

"Will that work?" I asked him, cautiously.

"Yes! If it's on. Where's his phone?" he asked.

"I don't know! It could be anywhere. If the police don't have it and it wasn't in his car or . . . oh man." I took a deep breath.

"What?" Jake asked, glancing over at me.

"I think I might know where it is."

"Yeah? Then let's go check!" He did a quick U-turn and headed back towards the city.

It felt as if the drive took forever even though we were at

my house in minutes. I rushed out of the car before it came to a complete stop and was in the house before Jake was out of the driver's seat. I all but ran into Kiowa's bedroom and threw open the closet door. I held my breath and stood on my toes, sliding a hand under the pile of sweaters on the top shelf. Yes! I grabbed the phone and met Jake at the door.

"Got it! Fingers crossed," I told him as he turned Kiowa's phone on and waited. It took eons for it to come on and then forever to get the home screen. Jake fiddled with it for an eternity and then looked over at me.

"So?" I asked, holding my breath.

A smile slowly lit up his face.

"It was on," he said triumphantly.

× × ×

Kiowa walked out of the Remand Centre wearing the same clothes he was arrested in. It had been a nightmare for him and he was pale, but as soon as he saw us, a huge smile lit up his face. My mother ran to Kiowa and threw her arms around him, crying while television and newspaper crews recorded our happy reunion. Kiowa hugged her tightly. Jake and I stood back and watched them, both of us smiling. We were getting my brother back! Kiowa looked over at me, and to my shock, tears started pouring down his face. He let go of my mom and took huge steps to reach me, grabbing me up in a hug that took my breath away.

"You did this, Feather," he said, hugging me tighter. He glanced up. "You too, Jake." He held out an arm to Jake and dragged him into the hug. "Thank you both." We hugged him back as reporters swarmed us.

"Kiowa, what do you think happened to Mia?" one asked, poking me with a microphone.

"Is Mia dead, Kiowa?" another asked. They were yelling questions as my mother herded us towards the car. We piled in and left the reporters behind as quickly as we could.

"I'll never be able to clear my name with them," Kiowa sighed. "No matter what, people will always wonder if I had something to do with Mia's disappearance."

"No they won't!" I told him. "They let you go!"

"I know they did. But you'll see. People will look at me with suspicion. They'll always wonder if I'm a killer," he said sadly.

Kiowa was right. From the moment he stepped out of the car at our house, there was something different about the way he was treated. Most people were kind. They welcomed him back and told him that they knew he was innocent. But there was always someone staring at him, crossing the street to avoid him or shielding their children from him as if he were a monster who was going to swoop in and grab them. Kiowa tried to keep a smile on his face, but the more it happened, the harder it was for him to pretend it didn't bother him. What tipped the scales for him was the morning he went out for a jog and found that someone had spray painted the word "killer" on his car. He came back red-faced and threw his phone across the room, shattering the screen.

"They're never going to leave me alone," he cried, sitting down hard at the table and dropping his head into his hands. I rushed to him and threw my arms around his neck.

"They're assholes, Ki." I hugged him hard. "You can't let them get to you."

"But they do get to me, Feather." He pulled back and looked at me. "I can't stay here."

"What are you talking about? This is our home," I said, my eyes filling with tears. "You can't leave."

"But I can't stay either," he said, willing me to understand. "If I stay here, I'll always be the guy who some people think killed his girlfriend."

I opened my mouth to respond but he held up his hand to stop me.

"I know, Feather. I hope she's not dead too. I loved her . . . *love* her," he amended. "But I can't stay."

"Where would you go?" I asked, wiping my eyes.

"I was thinking of transferring to the University of Toronto. They have a great medical school so I could finish my pre-med and stay there. No one would know me," he said. "I could start over."

"But you'd be in Toronto!"

He smiled.

"You could visit me whenever you want. Maybe you'll even go to school there."

I nodded. I didn't want my brother to wake up every day wondering if someone was going to paint the word "killer" on his car again.

"Okay," I told him. "Starting over sounds good."

He hugged me tightly.

"Thanks, Feather. I'll never be able to repay you for what you and Jake did to get me out of there."

"Just be happy," I told him.

CHAPTER 37
BLACKBIRD, FLY

He leaned on his shovel and took a deep breath, wiping a hand across his sweaty forehead. With the possibility of the river gone, this one had been particularly hard to get rid of. He sighed.

Once that Indian boy was out and they started to connect his girls, they'd be looking for him. There was a chance even the most inept police department — and so far, they all had varying degrees of ineptitude — would find him. As always, he'd move on. Find a new home. A new hunting ground.

It took him all night to pack up his belongings and load them into his truck. Even after he was done, it took another three hours to scrub down the entire house with bleach. His knees were sore and his back was tired but the house was spotless. You could eat off the floor, as his mother would have said. He looked over the house one more time but there was not one thing left that tied him to this house or to this city. He had told Michael that his mother was sick and he had to leave to care for her. No loose ends.

Time to move on.

He climbed into the cab of his truck and pulled out of the driveway, glancing into the rear-view mirror at the house where he had made so many memories.

He wished he had the time to finish. He missed his raven already. He ached with the thought of how she would have felt.

How she would have struggled.

How she would have died.

He drove quickly out of the city and accelerated to 120 as soon as he hit the highway. He was flying with Winnipeg fading rapidly behind him.

He smiled.

There would be other cities.

Other girls.

He glanced once more in the rear-view mirror, his gaze lingering a moment too long on the city retreating steadily behind him.

He missed seeing the motorcycle cutting across three lanes of traffic.

He missed seeing the transport truck in front of him slamming on its brakes to avoid hitting it and jackknifing right in front of him.

He looked forward when he heard the scream of brakes and slammed his own on, hitting the transport truck on an angle that sent his own truck rolling over and over across the highway.

He lost consciousness on the third roll.

He missed seeing a minivan plow into the driver's side of his truck.

He knew nothing again after that.

"I'm reporting from the scene of a major accident outside the city of Winnipeg, which occurred earlier this evening. Eyewitnesses report seeing a motorcycle cutting across several lanes of highway, causing a pileup that has so far taken the lives of seven people, including a family of four who were just starting a road trip that would have taken them across the country. We can confirm that the Trent family lost their lives on the highway this morning, along with fifty-one year old Lawrence Kent, who was a well-liked employee of a Winnipeg recreation centre. We will continue to follow this story as it unfolds this morning. Back to you, Mark."

EPILOGUE
ONE YEAR LATER

"Is my tie straight?" Kiowa walked into the kitchen, tugging at the neck of his Oxford shirt.

"Your tie is fine," I told him. "But your shirt isn't. You've got it buttoned wrong." I pointed at the tails of his shirt, hanging unevenly.

He fumbled with the buttons, undoing them and doing them back up. He glanced up at me.

"Better." I gave him a thumbs-up. "So, does it feel weird being back home?" He glanced up at me, still fiddling with his tie. He nodded slowly.

"Yeah. It does. I feel like I don't have a life here anymore. You know?" I nodded. "I've been in Toronto for almost a year. I like it there. I'm comfortable there. No one looks at me as if I'm guilty." He smiled wryly.

"I know." I grabbed his hand and squeezed it. "I've really missed you though."

"Me too," he said. "Is that better?" He faced me.

"Perfect." I smiled at him.

"Is Jake meeting us there?" he asked. I looked away.

"We broke up. He wasn't . . . as perfect as he seemed to be," I told him.

"Right. How's Matt doing?" Kiowa asked.

"He's good. Seeing someone at another school. He's happy."

"Good. I'm glad. And Ben?"

"He's okay." I smiled shyly. "We've been out a few times."

"What?" Kiowa looked surprised and then smiled. "I'm glad. You deserve someone nice, Feather. Ready?" He offered me his arm. I took it and spun under it so he was hugging me tightly.

"As I'll ever be," I told him, hugging him back.

"Then let's go."

× × ×

"We're here today to celebrate the life of our friend, Mia. You're here because you shared in her life. Because you loved her and because she loved you." Michael stood in front of the crowd and glanced over at a poster-sized photo of Mia Joseph, smiling at he camera. "Mia was so full of life. It's been a year since we lost our friend. But our memories of her have not dimmed. Our memories will never fade. Because Mia was a shining light for everyone who met her."

He paused and looked at the photo again. I wiped my eyes and looked over at my brother. His eyes were sad and I saw him take a hitching breath. I squeezed his hand tightly.

"Mia helped people. Whether it was taking care of her friends," he nodded towards me and Kiowa, "or sharing food with the homeless. Or giving up her bed so someone else could be comfortable. That was Mia." I nodded back. "If you see someone who needs help, honour Mia by lending a hand. Donate money. Donate your time. Do it in Mia's memory.

That's how we'll keep her alive." Michael gestured to the photo. He turned to the crowd again. "We won't forget her. Ever." He turned towards me. "Now, Mia's best friend would like to say a few words. Feather?"

I walked towards him, glancing at Mia's smile. I missed her as much now as I did a year ago when she disappeared. I still looked for her in crowds. I still thought it might be her every time my phone rang. I stood beside her picture and cleared my throat.

"Mia was my best friend from the first day we met. We were eight. A boy was bullying me on the playground and Mia punched him in the stomach." Laughter rang out around me. "And that's Mia. That *was* Mia. If she loved you, she was fiercely loyal. And I miss her every single day." I swallowed hard and looked at her photo. "I miss you, Mia. I will always miss you." I walked away before I started to cry. Kiowa enveloped me in a huge hug.

"I miss her too," he told me. "But I think she'd like this. Seeing so many people remembering her." I nodded.

"Yeah, she would. She'd love it."

"Do you want to get out of here?" he asked me.

"Yes, please." I took one last look at Mia's smiling face, silently saying goodbye before walking away.

Body of Aboriginal Girl Found in Local Park

The body of seventeen-year-old Lacey Howling Wolf was found last night in Confederation Park. Authorities are awaiting the results of an autopsy but foul play is suspected . . .

ABOUT THE AUTHOR

Melanie Florence is a full-time writer based in Toronto. She is the author of *Righting Canada's Wrongs: Residential Schools,* the SideStreets novel *One Night* and the Recordbooks title *Jordin Tootoo: The Highs and Lows in the Journey of the First Inuk to Play in the NHL,* which was chosen as an Honor Book by The American Indian Library Association. As a free-lance journalist, Melanie's byline has appeared in magazines including *Dance International, Writer, Parents Canada* and *Urban Male Magazine.* Melanie is of Plains Cree and Scottish descent.